THE
LEGEND
OF
SLEEPY
HOLLOW

睡谷傳奇

原著 _ Washington Irving 改寫 _ Janet Olearski 翻譯 _ 安卡斯

ABOUT THIS BOOK

For the Student

 Listen to the story and do some activities on your Audio CD.

 Talk about the story.

For the Teacher

Go to our Readers Resource site for information on using readers and downloadable Resource Sheets, photocopiable Worksheets, and Tapescripts. www.helblingreaders.com

For lots of great ideas on using Graded Readers consult Reading Matters, the Teacher's Guide to using Helbling Readers.

Structures

Sequencing of future tenses	• Could / was able to / managed to
Present perfect plus yet, already, just	• Had to / didn't have to
First conditional	• Shall / could for offers
Present and past passive	• May / can / could for permission • Might for future possibility
How long?	• Make and let
Very / really / quite	• Causative have • Want / ask / tell someone to do something

Structures from lower levels are also included.

CONTENTS

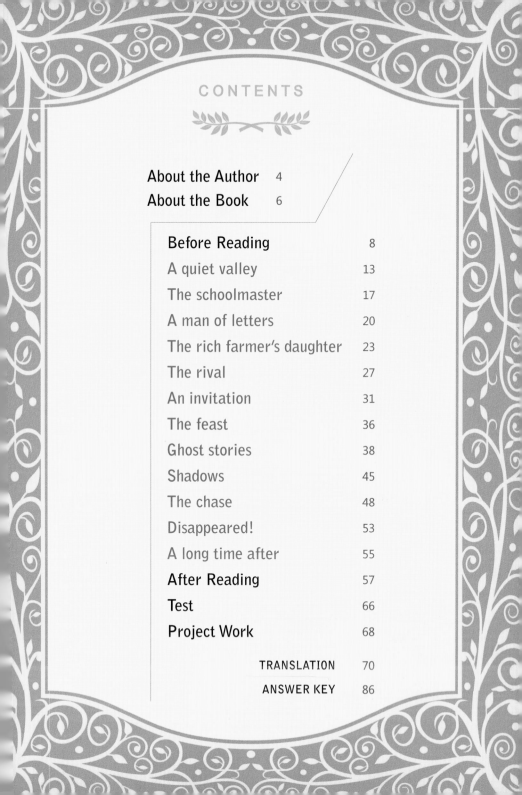

Washington Irving was born into a rich Scottish family in New York in 1783. He studied law but literature was his real passion. While he was working as a lawyer[1], he started to write for newspapers and magazines. His articles and stories satirized[2] the customs[3] and manners[4] of the Americans. New York was home to many Dutch settlers[5] and Irving wrote about them in his first book *A History of New York*, published in 1809. This humorous account by a fictional[6] character called Diedrich Knickerbocker was immensely successful and was described as 'the first great book of comic literature written by an American'.

In 1815 Irving moved to England to look after the family company, but the business was not a success and he returned to his writing. His most famous stories, *The Legend of Sleepy Hollow* and *Rip Van Winkle*, appeared in 1819. The popularity of these books made Irving a celebrity in Europe and America.

He lived in London, Paris and Madrid, writing stories, essays and history books, such as *Tales of a Traveler, The Life and Voyages of Christopher Columbus, The Conquest of Granada, Tales of the Alhambra*. He returned to New York in 1832 but ten years later he went back to Madrid in a diplomatic[7] role. He spent his last years in America, in Tarrytown in the valley of Sleepy Hollow where he wrote *The Life of George Washington*. He died there in 1859 at the age of 76.

1 lawyer [ˈlɔjɚ] (n.) 律師
2 satirize [ˈsætə,raɪz] (v.) 諷刺；挖苦
3 customs [ˈkʌstəmz] (n.)（作複數形）社會習俗
4 manners [ˈmænɚz] (n.)（作複數形）風俗習慣
5 settler [ˈsɛtlɚ] (n.) 移居者；移民者
6 fictional [ˈfɪkʃənḷ] (a.) 虛構的
7 diplomatic [,dɪpləˈmætɪk] (a.) 外交的
　（註：作者曾任美國駐西班牙大使）

The Legend of Sleepy Hollow (1809) tells the story of a schoolteacher from Connecticut, Ichabod Crane, who comes to the small village of Sleepy Hollow. When he meets Katrina Van Tassel, the pretty daughter of a wealthy farmer, he falls in love. But he has a rival, the boastful[1] Brom Bones. After a party at her house, Katrina rejects Ichabod's courtship[2] and he rides home dejected[3]. On the way back he encounters the terrifying Headless Horseman, the ghost of an enemy soldier from the Revolutionary War[4]. A frightening chase ensues and Ichabod disappears. The people of Sleepy Hollow believe that Ichabod's ghost now haunts the village.

The narration runs on various levels. The main story is presented as an authentic account found among the papers of the narrator, Diedrich Knickerbocker, a fictional Dutch historian. The stories about the war, ghosts and superstitions are told by the villagers. We know also that Ichabod reads some frightening stories from his favorite book, *A History of New England Witchcraft*.

The Legend of Sleepy Hollow is an early example of American fiction. It explores the themes typical of the newborn nation [5]: greed for money and possessions in a country rich in natural resources, physical mobility in a vast continent where people can travel to seek [6] their fortune, the survival of the European heritage, the memory of the war still fresh in people's minds and their attachment to the superstitions and beliefs of the past.

---

1 boastful [ˈbostfəl] (a.) 臭屁的
2 courtship [ˈkortʃɪp] (n.) 追求
3 dejected [dɪˈdʒɛktɪd] (a.) 沮喪的；挹鬱的
4 Revolutionary War 指美國的獨立戰爭（1775-1783）
5 newborn nation 新獨立的國家
　（指於 1776 年宣布獨立的美國）
6 seek [sik] (v.) 尋求

1 Match the words and the pictures.

_____ ① ghost   _____ ④ witch
_____ ② dragon   _____ ⑤ goblin
_____ ③ giant   _____ ⑥ headless horseman

2 Complete the sentences with the words above.

ⓐ A _____ mixes ingredients in a big pot or cauldron to make magic potions.

ⓑ A _____ is huge. It has got wings and a long tail.

ⓒ A _____ is an enormous person.

ⓓ The _____ was killed on the battlefield and his ghost still rides his horse.

ⓔ A _____ appears after death and usually haunts old castles.

ⓕ A _____ is a bold little creature that plays tricks on people.

3 Look at these pictures from the story. Write six questions about them. Exchange questions with your partner. Write answers to your partner's questions. Keep your answers in a safe place until after you read the story.

4 You are going to read about the following places in the story. Do some research on the Internet and write a sentence about each of them.

Tarry Town   The Hudson River   Sleepy Hollow

5 What do you think *The Legend of Sleepy Hollow* will be about? Tick (✓) below.

____ (a) A place where people keep falling asleep.
____ (b) A poor man who becomes rich.
____ (c) A ghost story.
____ (d) A war story.
____ (e) A story about love and romance.
____ (f) A story about people who tell stories.

6 Here are the pictures of three characters from the story. Listen to their descriptions and number the pictures.

Brom Van Brunt

Ichabod Crane

Baltus Van Tassel

7 Think about the following and answer the questions.

_____ a Which of these things is <u>not</u> usually in a classroom?
   1 copybooks   2 books   3 inkstands
   4 a mirror   5 a desk   6 windows

_____ b Which of these is <u>not</u> a farmer's job?
   1 take the horses to water
   2 cut wood for the winter fire
   3 drive the cows from pasture
   4 make hay
   5 mend fences
   6 rock a cradle

_____ c Which animal is <u>not</u> usually found in a farmyard?
   1 pig   2 ostrich   3 pigeon
   4 turkey   5 goose   6 hen

_____ d Circle two items you can wear on your head.

   coat   stockings   breeches   cap   gown
   petticoat   straw hat   shoes   dress   buttons

8 Match the words from the story with the pictures.

_____ a crane   _____ e cradle
_____ b logs   _____ f pumpkins
_____ c beehive   _____ g fiddle
_____ d scarecrow   _____ h sword

9 Use each of these words to complete the following sentences.

a The teacher's clothes fluttered in the wind, frightening the birds, so that from a distance he looked like a _____.

b The musician played his _____ and everyone danced.

c Since Ichabod was tall, but extremely thin, with narrow shoulders, people thought he looked like a _____.

d Ichabod sat for hours with a child on one knee and rocking a baby in a _____ at the same time with one foot.

e Mrs Van Tassel was a good cook and she could make tasty pies from _____.

f The bees lived in a large _____ at the bottom of the garden.

g Ichabod's schoolhouse was one large room, built with _____ from the forest.

h While Ichabod was riding the _____ slipped from under him.

A QUIET VALLEY

*The following account[1] was found among
the papers of the late[2] Diedrich Knickerbocker.*

On the eastern shore of the Hudson River there is a small town called Greensburgh. This place is better known as Tarry Town. It was given this name by the wives of that area because on market days their husbands 'tarried,' or wasted time, at the local tavern[3]. I cannot confirm this myself but I mention[4] it just to be precise.

There is a little valley surrounded by high hills about two miles from here. This is one of the quietest places in the whole world. A small stream glides[5] through it so silently that it could lull[6] one to sleep. Only the sound of the birds ever interrupts this tranquility.

I remember that, when I was very young, I once wandered into a grove[7] of trees. It was noon, when all nature is strangely quiet. The trees shaded one side of the valley. I couldn't think of a better place than this little valley where I could escape from the world and its distractions, and quietly dream away the remnants[8] of a troubled[9] life.

---

1 account [əˈkaʊnt] (n.) 描述；報導
2 late [let] (a.) 已故的
3 tavern [ˈtævɚn] (n.) 小酒館
4 mention [ˈmɛnʃən] (v.) 提及
5 glide [glaɪd] (v.) 緩緩流過
6 lull [lʌl] (v.) 使安靜；使入睡
7 grove [grov] (n.) 小樹林；樹叢
8 remnant [ˈrɛmnənt] (n.) 殘餘
9 troubled [ˈtrʌbl̩d] (a.) 紛擾的

COUNTRY LIFE AND CITY LIFE

- Do you live in the country or in a city?
- Where would you prefer to live – the countryside or the city? Why?

Because of the lazy atmosphere of the place and the character of its inhabitants, who are descended from the original Dutch settlers, this valley has been known for a long time by the name of Sleepy Hollow[1]. The young men who live here are called the Sleepy Hollow Boys. A drowsy[2], dreamy influence seems to hang over the land. Supposedly, a German doctor put a spell[3] on the place during the early days of the settlement.

According to another story an old Indian chief held his powwows[4] here. Certainly something seems to have cast[5] a spell over the minds of the good people. They have all kinds of strange beliefs. They go into trances[6], have visions, frequently see strange sights, and hear music and voices in the air. The whole neighborhood is full of stories of superstitions[7] and haunted[8] places.

However, one dominant spirit haunts this magical region. It is the apparition[9] of a figure on horseback, without a head. Some people think it is the ghost of a soldier whose head was carried away by a cannon ball in a battle during the Revolutionary War. The local people often see him hurrying along in the dark of night. He haunts not just the valley, but the adjacent roads and a nearby church.

---

1 hollow [ˈhɑlo] (n.) 山谷
2 drowsy [ˈdrauzɪ] (a.) 昏昏欲睡的
3 spell [spɛl] (n.) 咒語；魔咒
4 powwow [ˈpau͵wau] (n.) 巫師；巫術儀式
5 cast [kæst] (v.) 投下
6 trance [træns] (n.) 恍神；催眠狀態
7 superstition [͵supəˈstɪʃən] (n.) 迷信
8 haunted [ˈhɔntɪd] (a.) 鬧鬼的
9 apparition [͵æpəˈrɪʃən] (n.) 幽靈

According to historians the soldier's body was buried in the churchyard and his ghost now rides to the scene of battle in a nightly search for his missing head. It seems he sometimes rushes with great speed through the Hollow because he is in a hurry to get back to the churchyard before daybreak.

This legend has provided material for many wild stories, and at all the country firesides he is known by the name of the Headless Horseman of Sleepy Hollow.

THE HEADLESS HORSEMAN

- How did the horseman lose his head?
- Which places does he haunt?
- What is he searching for?
- When must he return to the churchyard?

1 inhale [ɪn`hel] (v.) 吸入
2 crane [kren] (n.) 鶴
3 dangle [`dæŋgl̩] (v.) 懸蕩；吊
4 shovel [`ʃʌvl̩] (n.) 鏟子；鐵鍬
5 stride [straɪd] (v.) 大步走；跨過
6 flutter [`flʌtɚ] (v.) 飄揚；振翅
7 scarecrow [`skɛr͵kro] (n.) 稻草人
8 log [lɔg] (n.) 圓木；原木
9 glaze [glez] (v.) 裝配玻璃
10 twig [twɪg] (n.) 細枝；嫩枝
11 stake [stek] (n.) 樁

THE SCHOOLMASTER

[5] It is not just the local people who imagine things. Everyone who comes to live in the area is affected. However wide awake they were before they arrived in this sleepy region, they soon inhale[1] the magic influence of the air and begin to imagine things. In these little Dutch valleys everything stays the same. It has been many years since I visited Sleepy Hollow, but I'm sure everything has remained exactly as it was.

Around thirty years ago, a man from Connecticut by the name of Ichabod Crane stayed or, as he expressed it, 'tarried' in Sleepy Hollow, for the purpose of instructing the children of the neighborhood. The surname of Crane[2] suited him. He was tall, but extremely thin, with narrow shoulders, long arms and legs. His hands dangled[3] a mile out of his sleeves, and his feet were like shovels[4]. His head was small and flat on the top. He had huge ears, large green glassy eyes, and a long nose. If you saw him striding[5] across a hill on a windy day, with his clothes fluttering[6] around him, you could have mistaken him for a scarecrow[7].

His schoolhouse was one large room, constructed from logs[8]. The windows were partly glazed[9], and partly covered up with pages from old copybooks. When not in use, the room was locked by twisting a twig[10] in the handle of the door, and by leaning stakes[11] against the window shutters.

It was easy for a thief to get in, but it was likely to be difficult for him to get out again. The schoolhouse was in a lonely but attractive location at the foot of a woody hill. There was a stream close by with a large birch[1] tree growing at one end.

From there the low murmur of his pupils' voices, studying their lessons, could be heard on drowsy summer days, like the hum of a beehive. This was interrupted now and then by Ichabod's authoritative[2] voice, speaking in a tone of menace[3], or by the terrible sound of the birch, as he encouraged some tardy[4] loiterer[5] to move along the flowery[6] path of knowledge.

I am not saying that he was a cruel man. On the contrary, he only used the birch on the real troublemakers[7]. He never punished anyone without assuring him afterwards, 'you will remember and thank me for this as long as you live.'

SCHOOL

- What is your school like?
- How many classrooms are there?
- Have you got a library, a sports hall or a swimming pool at your school?
- Do you have lunch at school? If so, where do you eat?
- How many students are there at your school?

1 birch [bɜtʃ] (n.) 樺樹	6 flowery [ˈflauərɪ] (a.) 豐富多彩的
2 authoritative [əˈθɔrə,tetɪv] (a.) 權威性的	7 troublemaker [ˈtrʌbl̩,mekɚ] (n.) 鬧事者；搗蛋鬼
3 menace [ˈmɛnɪs] (n.) 威脅；恐嚇	8 revenue [ˈrɛvə,nju] (n.) 收入
4 tardy [ˈtɑrdɪ] (a.) 慢吞吞的	9 dilating [daɪˈletɪŋ] (a.) 膨脹的
5 loiterer [ˈlɔɪtərə] (n.) 閒晃者	10 anaconda [,ænəˈkɑndə] (n.) 蟒蛇

When school was over, he usually accompanied some of the smaller boys home if they had pretty sisters, or if their mothers were good cooks. He took care to be on good terms with his pupils. The revenue[8] from his school was small, and it was scarcely enough to feed him. He ate a lot and though he was thin he had the dilating[9] powers of an anaconda[10].

To help out with his maintenance, he lived and ate at the houses of the farmers whose children he taught. He lived a week at a time with each family, thus going the rounds[11] of the neighborhood with all his worldly belongings tied up in a cotton handkerchief.

So that this was not too costly for his patrons, who considered the cost of schooling a heavy burden[12], he made himself useful. He helped the farmers with light work, helped to make hay, mended fences, took the horses to water, drove the cows from pasture[13], and cut wood for the winter fire. He found favor in the eyes of the mothers by being nice to the children, particularly the youngest. He sat for hours with a child on one knee, rocking a cradle[14] at the same time with his other foot.

Ichabod was also the neighborhood singing master and earned a few shillings by instructing the children to sing hymns[15]. On Sundays, he went to church with his group of chosen singers, and his voice resounded[16] far above the rest of the congregation[17].

11 round [raʊnd] (n.) 兜一圈
12 burden [ˋbɝdn] (n.) 負擔
13 pasture [ˋpæstʃɚ] (n.) 牧草地
14 cradle [ˋkredl] (n.) 搖籃
15 hymn [hɪm] (n.) 聖歌
16 resound [rɪˋzaʊnd] (v.) 發出回響
17 congregation [͵kɑŋgrɪˋgeʃən] (n.) 會眾

A MAN OF LETTERS

A schoolmaster is generally a man of some importance in female circles[1]. He is considered to be a kind of idle[2] gentleman, with taste and accomplishments[3] superior to those of the rough country boys. Our man of letters enjoyed the smiles of all the young country ladies. Between church services on Sundays, he was the centre of their attention, gathering grapes for them from the vines in the churchyard and reading aloud for their amusement the epitaphs[4] written on the tombstones. Sometimes he walked along the bank of the pond with a whole bevy[5] of them. The shy country boys hung back[6], envying[7] his superior elegance and style of conversation.

Ichabod was a kind of travelling newspaper. He carried the local gossip from house to house so his appearance was always greeted with satisfaction. The women regarded him as a man of great learning because he read books all the way through, and he was an expert in Cotton Mather's book 'History of New England Witchcraft[8],' in which, by the way, he firmly[9] believed.

POPULARITY

- Why do you think Ichabod is so popular?
- What advice can you give to someone who wants to be popular?

1 circle ['sɜkl] (n.) 圈子
2 idle ['aɪdl] (a.) 悠閒的
3 accomplishment [ə'kɑmplɪʃmənt] (n.) 成就
4 epitaph ['ɛpə,tæf] (n.) 墓誌銘
5 bevy ['bɛvɪ] (n.) 一群
6 hang back 退縮；猶豫
7 envy ['ɛnvɪ] (v.) 妒忌；羨慕
8 witchcraft ['wɪtʃ,kræft] (n.) 巫術
9 firmly ['fɜmlɪ] (adv.) 堅定地
10 crafty ['kræftɪ] (a.) 狡猾的
11 credulous ['krɛdʒʊləs] (a.) 易受騙的

He was both crafty[10] and credulous[11]. No tale was too monstrous for him to believe. After school he loved to stretch himself out on the bank of the stream by his schoolhouse and read old Mather's frightening tales until the arrival of evening made the printed page a mist[12] before his eyes. Then, as he walked home through woods to the farmhouse where he was staying, every little sound at that witching[13] hour stirred his imagination and frightened him.

On such occasions, either to stop himself from thinking or to drive away evil spirits, he sang hymns. As the good people of Sleepy Hollow sat by their doors in the evening, they were often surprised to hear him singing on a distant hill or on the dark road.

Ichabod spent the long winter evenings with the old women, listening to their tales of ghosts and goblins[14]. As they sat spinning[15] by the fire, they told him about haunted fields, and haunted streams, and haunted bridges, and haunted houses, and particularly about the Headless Horseman of the Hollow.

In return he entertained them with his stories of witchcraft. He frightened them with tales about omens[16] and terrible sights and sounds, and speculation[17] about the significance of certain comets and shooting stars. He enjoyed all this while he was sitting comfortably by the fire, but then he paid for it when he had to walk home alone.

---

12 mist [mɪst] (n.) 薄霧
13 witching [ˈwɪtʃɪŋ] (a.) 蠱惑的
14 goblin [ˈgɑblɪn] (n.) 醜惡的妖怪
15 spin [spɪn] (v.) 紡織
16 omen [ˈomən] (n.) 預兆；徵兆
17 speculation [ˌspɛkjəˈleʃən] (n.) 推測

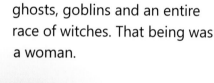

Everywhere he saw fearful shapes in the ghastly[1] glare[2] of the snowy night. Every shrub[3] covered with snow looked like a ghost waiting for him on the path. He was terrified by the sound of his own steps. He dreaded[4] to look over his shoulder in case he saw somebody walking close behind him. Whenever the wind howled through the trees, it seemed to him to be the galloping[5] horseman on one of his nightly rides.

Daylight put an end to all these evils. But, then, one day Ichabod's path was crossed by a being[6] who causes more trouble to mortal man than ghosts, goblins and an entire race of witches. That being was a woman.

1 ghastly [ˈgæstlɪ] (a.) 恐怖的　　4 dread [drɛd] (v.) 懼怕
2 glare [glɛr] (n.) 刺眼的強光　　5 galloping [ˈgæləpɪŋ] (a.) 飛馳的
3 shrub [ʃrʌb] (n.) 矮樹；灌木　　6 being [ˈbiɪŋ] (n.) 人；生物

THE RICH FARMER'S DAUGHTER

Among the musical pupils who came one evening a week for instruction was Katrina Van Tassel. She was the only child of a well-off[7] Dutch farmer. She was a fine healthy girl of eighteen, plump[8] and rosy-cheeked, like one of her father's peaches. She was also a bit of a flirt[9], which you could tell from the way she dressed. She wore ornaments of pure gold, and her petticoat[10] was short so that she showed off the prettiest foot and ankle in the countryside. Ichabod Crane had a soft and foolish heart towards young women so it is not surprising that such a tasty morsel[11] soon found favor in his eyes.

Katrina's father, old Baltus Van Tassel, was only concerned with his own farm, where everything was snug[12] and happy. He did not lead an extravagant life but he had everything he needed.

His home was on the banks of the Hudson, in a green and fertile place. An elm tree spread its branches over a spring of the sweetest water. Close to the farmhouse there was a vast barn and every corner of it seemed to burst with the treasures of the farm. Swallows[13] and martins[14] flew twittering around the eaves[15], and rows of cooing pigeons enjoyed the sunshine on the roof. Fat pigs grunted in the comfort of their pens[16]. There were geese in the pond and turkeys, cockerels and hens in the farmyard.

---

7 well-off [ˈwɛlˈɔf] (a.) 富有的
8 plump [plʌmp] (a.) 豐滿的
9 flirt [flɜt] (n.) 賣弄風情的人
10 petticoat [ˈpɛtɪˌkot] (n.) 襯裙
11 morsel [ˈmɔrsl] (n.) 佳餚

12 snug [snʌg] (a.) 舒適的
13 swallow [ˈswɑlo] (n.) 燕子
14 martin [ˈmɑrtɪn] (n.) 岩燕
15 eaves [ivz] (n.) 簷；簷
16 pen [pɛn] (n.) 獸欄

Ichabod's mouth watered as he looked at this rich promise of luxurious winter food. He imagined pigeon pie, geese in gravy[1], and ducks in dishes, covered in onion sauce. Instead of the pigs he saw slices of bacon, and juicy ham. Instead of turkey he saw a roast bird with a necklace of savory[2] sausages.

Ichabod rolled his great green eyes over the fat meadow lands, the rich fields of wheat, of rye[3], of buckwheat[4], of Indian corn, and the orchards full of fruit, which surrounded Van Tassel's home, and his heart longed for[5] the young woman who was to inherit these lands. He imagined selling everything, and investing the money in land. He imagined himself married to Katrina and with a whole family of children, all of them traveling in a wagon loaded with household items. He saw himself riding a fine horse, setting out for a new life in Kentucky, Tennessee – or who knows where!

When he entered the house, the conquest of his heart was complete. It was a spacious farmhouse, with a sloping[6] roof, built in the style of the first Dutch settlers. Farming and fishing equipment was stored under the eaves of the house. There was a spinning wheel[7] at one end of the house, and a churn[8] at the other, showing the different uses to which the porch[9] was put.

In the hall, arranged on a dresser[10], there were rows of glittering[11] pewter[12]. In one corner stood a huge bag of wool ready to be spun. In another corner, cloth, Indian corn, and dried apples and peaches, hung in sacks along the walls. Through the open parlor door he saw carved chairs, and dark wood tables shining like mirrors. Colored birds' eggs were suspended above the mantelpiece[13], a great ostrich egg was hung from the centre of the room, and a cupboard displayed silver ornaments and china[14] plates.

LOVE

- Do you think Ichabod has fallen in love with Katrina?
- Why does he want to marry her?

1 gravy [ˋɡrevɪ] (n.) 肉汁
2 savory [ˋsevərɪ] (a.) 美味的
3 rye [raɪ] (n.) 黑麥
4 buckwheat [ˋbʌk͵hwit] (n.) 蕎麥
5 long for 渴望……
6 sloping [ˋslopɪŋ] (a.) 傾斜的
7 spinning wheel 紡車
8 churn [tʃɝn] (n.) 攪乳器
9 porch [portʃ] (n.) 門廊；入口處
10 dresser [ˋdrɛsɚ] (n.) 餐具櫥
11 glittering [ˋɡlɪtərɪŋ] (a.) 閃閃發光的
12 pewter [ˋpjutɚ] (n.) 白鑞器
13 mantelpiece [ˋmæntl͵pis] (n.) 壁爐架
14 china [ˋtʃaɪnə] (n.) 瓷器

From the moment Ichabod laid his eyes on the house and its contents, he lost his peace of mind. His only thought was how to gain the affections of Van Tassel's daughter. This posed[1] more difficulties than those encountered[2] by a knight in a fairytale.

A knight only had to deal with[3] giants, witches and dragons. It was easy to defeat all of these. He only had to reach the castle dungeon[4], where the lady of his heart was imprisoned. A knight could do this as easily as cutting into a pie, and then the lady gave him her hand as a matter of course[5].

Ichabod, on the contrary, had to win the heart of a spoilt[6] young country girl, whose whims[7] were always presenting him with new difficulties. He had to meet real flesh and blood[8] rivals, her many admirers, who opened every door to her heart, who watched each other angrily and who were ready to take action against any new competitor.

---

1 pose [poz] (v.) 造成；引起
2 encounter [ɪnˈkaʊntɚ] (v.) 遭遇
3 deal with 應付
4 dungeon [ˈdʌndʒən] (n.) 地牢
5 as a matter of course 照例；不用説
6 spoilt [spɔɪlt] (a.) 被寵壞的
7 whim [wɪm] (n.) 奇想；異想
8 flesh and blood 血肉之軀

THE RIVAL

The most impressive of these was a strong, energetic young man, called Abraham or, according to the Dutch abbreviation, Brom.

Brom Van Brunt was a local hero. The countryside was full of stories of his feats[9] of strength. He was broad-shouldered and agile, with short curly black hair. His face was not unpleasant, with a mixed expression of fun and arrogance. People gave him the nickname of Brom Bones because of his Herculean[10] frame[11] and powerful limbs[12]. He was famous for his great knowledge of horsemanship, and was as skillful[13] on horseback as a Tartar[14]. He always won races and cock[15] fights, and because of his strength he was the judge in all disputes[16]. No one ever argued against his decisions.

Brom was a rough type but he was good-humored. He had three or four close companions, who regarded him as their model. With them he traveled around the countryside getting into fights or having a good time. In cold weather he always wore a fur cap with a fox's tail, and when people spotted this hat from a distance, among a group of horse riders, they knew a storm[17] was coming. Sometimes his gang rode past the farmhouses at midnight, whooping and shouting. Old ladies, startled[18] out of their sleep, exclaimed, 'There goes Brom Bones and his gang!'

9 feat [fit] (n.) 功績；偉業
10 Herculean [hɝˋkjuliən] (a.) 力大無比的
11 frame [frem] (n.) 身形
12 limb [lɪm] (n.) (四) 肢
13 skillful [ˋskɪlfəl] (a.) 熟練的
14 Tartar [ˋtɑrtɚ] (n.) 韃靼人
15 cock [kɑk] (n.) 公雞
16 dispute [dɪˋspjut] (n.) 爭論
17 storm [stɔrm] (n.) 風暴；動盪
18 startle [ˋstɑrtl] (v.) 驚駭；吃驚

The neighbors regarded him with a mixture of awe[1], admiration, and good-will. Whenever any prank[2] or brawl[3] occurred in the vicinity, they always shook their heads, and agreed that Brom Bones must be the cause of it.

Brom chose the beautiful Katrina as the object of his attention. Though his romantic advances were more like those of a bear, Katrina did not completely discourage his hopes. When Brom's horse was seen tied up outside Van Tassel's house on a Sunday night, it was a sure sign that its master was inside courting[4] Katrina. All other suitors[5] passed by in despair without stopping. They didn't want to upset[6] a lovesick[7] lion.

This was the formidable[8] rival with whom Ichabod Crane was in competition. Braver men avoided contests like these. Wiser men despaired[9] of them. But in his character Ichabod had a mixture of flexibility and perseverance[10]. Though he bent, he never broke, and though he bowed beneath the slightest pressure, the moment the pressure was off, he stood up straight and carried his head as high as ever.

It was madness for him to compete openly with his rival. Ichabod did not like to be beaten in love, so he made his advances in a quiet and crafty manner. As a singing master, he made frequent visits to the farmhouse. There was no need for him to worry about interference from the parents, which is so often a obstacle in the path of lovers.

Baltus Van Tassel was an easy-going man. He loved his daughter even better than his pipe and, like a reasonable man and an excellent father, he let her do anything she liked. His wife had enough to attend to in the house and farmyard. As she wisely observed, ducks and geese are foolish and must be looked after, but girls can take care of themselves.

PARENTS

- What qualities must a mother and a father have to be good parents?
- Are Baltus and his wife good parents?
- Do you have any special advice for them about Katrina?

So, while Katrina's mother worked at her spinning wheel at one end of the porch, Baltus sat smoking his pipe at the other. In the meantime, Ichabod sat with Katrina by the side of the stream under the great elm, or strolled[11] with her in the twilight[12], that hour so favorable to romance.

I admit I do not know how women's hearts are wooed[13] and won. To me they have always been a mystery. Some seem to have only one door of access[14], while others have thousands, and can be captured in many different ways. From the moment Ichabod Crane made his advances, Brom Bones seemed to lose interest. His horse was no longer seen tied up outside the house on Sunday nights, and a deadly[15] feud[16] gradually arose between him and the schoolmaster.

---

1 awe [ɔ] (n.) 畏怯
2 prank [præŋk] (n.) 惡作劇
3 brawl [brɔl] (n.) 爭吵
4 court [kort] (v.) 追求；獻殷勤
5 suitor [ˈsutə] (n.) 追求者
6 upset [ʌpˈsɛt] (v.) 攪亂
7 lovesick [ˈlʌvˌsɪk] (a.) 害相思病的
8 formidable [ˈfɔrmɪdəbl] (a.) 難對付的

9 despair [dɪˈspɛr] (v.) 不抱希望
10 perseverance [ˌpɜsəˈvɪrəns] (n.) 堅持不懈
11 stroll [strol] (v.) 散步；閒逛
12 twilight [ˈtwaɪˌlaɪt] (n.) 黃昏
13 woo [wu] (v.) 追求
14 access [ˈæksɛs] (n.) 通道
15 deadly [ˈdɛdlɪ] (a.) 致命的
16 feud [fjud] (n.) 宿怨

Brom liked the idea of settling[1] their dispute over the lady in combat[2], like the knights of old. But Ichabod was too conscious of his opponent's superior strength to enter into a fight with him. He was not going to give him any opportunity to try.

Brom found Ichabod's pacifism[3] very irritating. He had no alternative but to think up some unpleasant practical joke to play on his rival. Ichabod became an object of persecution[4] for Brom and his gang. Until this time his life was very peaceful, but now they caused him all kinds of trouble. They blocked the chimney of his school so that it filled with smoke. They broke in[5] at night, in spite of Ichabod's clever security precautions, and turned everything topsy-turvy[6]. The poor schoolmaster began to think all the witches in the country held their meetings there.

PRACTICAL JOKES

- What is a practical joke?
- What practical jokes did Brom and his friends play on Ichabod?
- Have you ever played a practical joke on anyone? What did you do?

Brom took every opportunity to ridicule[7] Ichabod in Katrina's presence. He even taught a dog to whine[8], and introduced it as a rival of Ichabod's who was there to instruct her in hymn singing. This went on for some time without either of them winning.

---

1 settle ['sɛtl] (v.) 解決;清算
2 combat ['kɑmbæt] (n.) 決鬥;格鬥
3 pacifism ['pæsə,fɪzəm] (n.) 和平主義
4 persecution [,pɜsɪ'kjuʃən] (n.) 迫害
5 break in 闖入
6 topsy-turvy ['tɑpsɪ't3vɪ] (adv.) 顛倒地
7 ridicule ['rɪdɪkjul] (v.) 嘲笑;揶揄
8 whine [hwaɪn] (v.) (狗等) 發哀鳴聲

AN INVITATION

One autumn afternoon Ichabod was sitting in his classroom watching his students at work when the silence was interrupted by the arrival of one of Van Tassel's servants. He came riding up to the school door with an invitation for Ichabod to attend a party that evening at Van Tassel's house.

The schoolroom was now full of noise and activity. The students were rushed through their lessons. Those who were fast managed to get through their lesson without being punished. Those who were slow got a smack[9] on their rear[10] to speed them up or help them understand a long word.

Books were thrown aside without being put away on the shelves, inkstands[11] were upset[12], benches were pushed over, and the whole school was turned loose[13] an hour before the usual time. The students burst out of the schoolhouse and onto the grass like an army of young imps[14], yelping[15] and making a racket[16].

Ichabod spent an extra half hour getting ready, brushing dust off his best black suit – indeed, his only black suit - and combing his hair in the schoolhouse's broken old mirror. He wanted to appear before Katrina in the true style of a cavalier so he borrowed a horse from the farmer with whom he was lodged[17], an old Dutchman called Hans Van Ripper.

9　smack [smæk] (n.) 一巴掌
10　rear [rɪr] (n.) 臀部
11　inkstand [ˋɪŋkˌstænd] (n.) 墨水瓶架
12　upset [ʌpˋsɛt] (v.) 打翻
13　turn loose　打發回家

14　imp [ɪmp] (n.) 頑童
15　yelp [jɛlp] (v.) 叫喊
16　racket [ˋrækɪt] (n.) 喧譁
17　lodge [lɑdʒ] (v.) 暫住；寄宿

He made his way to the party on horseback like a knight in search of adventure.

It is only fair to give you a true description of my hero and his horse. The animal he was riding was a broken-down bad-tempered[1] work horse. He was thin and ugly. His head was shaped like a hammer[2]. His mane and tail were tangled[3] and full of burs[4]. He was blind in one eye and that eye seemed to look angrily at you, while the other eye had the look of a devil in it. He was called Gunpowder and, judging by that name he once must have been a very ferocious animal. In fact he once was a favorite horse of his master Van Ripper, who was a mad horse rider. Very probably some of Van Ripper's own spirit was infused into the animal. Gunpowder looked old and broken-down, but in reality he had an evil character inside him.

Ichabod rode with short stirrups[5], which brought his knees nearly up to the top of the saddle. His sharp elbows stuck out like a grasshopper's[6] legs. He carried his whip vertically in his hand and, as his horse jogged[7] on, the motion of his arms was a bit like the flapping of a pair of wings. A small wool hat rested on the top of his nose, and the skirts of his black coat fluttered out almost to the horse's tail. Such was the ridiculous appearance of Ichabod and his horse.

As Ichabod rode, he thought of all the delights of autumn: the apples made into cider[8], the corn made into cakes, the pumpkins made into delicious pies, and the buckwheat made into breads. Katrina, with her delicate little hands, was going to cover those breads with butter and honey specially for him.

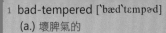

1 bad-tempered [`bæd`tɛmpɚd]
  (a.) 壞脾氣的
2 hammer [`hæmɚ] (n.) 鎚子

3 tangle [`tæŋgl̩] (v.) 糾結；糾纏
4 bur [bɝ] (n.) 附著之物
5 stirrup [`stɝəp] (n.) 馬鐙
6 grasshopper [`græs,hɑpɚ] (n.) 蚱蜢
7 jog [dʒɑg] (v.) 慢跑
8 cider [`saɪdɚ] (n.) 蘋果酒；蘋果汁

[20] His head was full of sweet thoughts like these as he travelled along the hillside overlooking the Hudson River. As the sun set, just a few amber[1] clouds floated in the sky, without a breath of air to move them. The golden horizon changed gradually into a pure apple green, and from that into a deep blue.

Towards the evening Ichabod arrived at the Van Tassel residence, which he found full of all the best people from the surrounding countryside. There were old farmers wearing homemade coats and breeches[2], blue stockings, and huge shoes with magnificent pewter buckles[3]. Their wives wore caps, long gowns, and homemade petticoats. There were young women, almost as old-fashioned as their mothers, except where a straw hat, a fine ribbon, or perhaps a white dress, gave evidence of city innovation[4]. The sons wore short coats, with rows of stupendous[5] brass[6] buttons, and their hair styled in the fashion of the times.

COLORS

- The author uses different colors and tones to describe people, places and things in the story. What do these colors describe?

apple green	silver	black	white
deep blue	golden	amber	blue

Brom Bones, however, was the hero of the scene. He came to the gathering on his favorite horse Daredevil, a creature, like himself, full of mischief[7], and which only Brom could control. Brom was, in fact, noted for preferring nasty[8] animals. His horses played all kinds of tricks and kept the rider in constant risk of breaking his neck. In Brom's opinion, a well-behaved horse was unworthy[9] of a lad[10] of spirit.

1 amber [ˋæmbɚ] (a.) 琥珀色的
2 breeches [ˋbrɪtʃɪz] (n.) 馬褲
3 buckle [ˋbʌkl̩] (n.) 釦子
4 innovation [ˏɪnəˋveʃən] (n.) 革新
5 stupendous [stjuˋpɛndəs] (a.) 巨大的

6 brass [bræs] (a.) 黃銅製的
7 mischief [ˋmɪstʃɪfɪ] (n.) 頑皮；惡作劇
8 nasty [ˋnæstɪ] (a.) 難纏的
9 unworthy [ʌnˋwɝðɪ] (a.) 不配的
10 lad [læd] (n.) 青年；少年

THE FEAST

When Ichabod entered the Van Tassel mansion he was overcome[1] by what he saw. He wasn't impressed by the sight of all those beautiful young women, but by the huge display of cakes of various kinds.

There were doughnuts, sweet cakes, shortcake, ginger cakes, honey cakes, and the whole family of cakes. Then there were apple pies, and peach pies, and pumpkin pies. There were slices of ham and smoked beef, and delectable[2] dishes of preserved plums, and pears, and quinces[3], not to mention roasted chickens, together with bowls of milk and cream, all mixed up higgledy-piggledy[4]. And in the middle of the table sending up clouds of vapor was the teapot. Ichabod Crane managed to do justice to every dainty[5].

Ichabod's spirits rose when he ate good food. As he ate he could not help looking all around him with large greedy eyes, chuckling[6] at the possibility that he might one day be lord of all this luxury and splendor. He looked forward to turning his back on[7] the old schoolhouse, and saying goodbye to Hans Van Ripper, and every other mean person like him.

Old Baltus Van Tassel moved about among his guests with a face full of good humor. He shook hands with his guests, gave them a friendly slap on the shoulder, laughed loudly and invited them to 'carry on[8] and help yourselves'. The sound of music summoned everyone to the dance. The grey-haired musician's fiddle[9] was as old and battered[10] as himself. He played on just two or three strings, accompanying every movement of his bow with a motion of the head, bowing almost to the ground, and stamping with his foot whenever a new couple entered the dance.

Ichabod prided himself on[11] his dancing as much as his vocal powers[12]. No part of him was idle. His body was in full motion, clattering[13] about the room. Everyone, including the farm workers, came to admire him and stood looking with delight at the scene through the open doors and windows. So, this man who usually spent his time beating naughty boys was now animated and joyous. The lady of his heart was his partner in the dance, smiling graciously in reply to all his loving looks. Meanwhile Brom Bones, who was overcome with[14] love and jealousy, sat brooding[15] by himself in a corner.

1 overcome [ˌovəˈkʌm] (v.) 征服
2 delectable [dɪˈlɛktəbl] (a.) 美味的
3 quince [kwɪns] (n.) 溫桲果
4 higgledy-piggledy [ˈhɪɡldɪˈpɪɡldɪ] (adv.) 亂七八糟地
5 dainty [ˈdentɪ] (n.) 佳肴
6 chuckle [ˈtʃʌkl] (v.) 咯咯笑
7 turn one's back on 掉頭離開
8 carry on 繼續
9 fiddle [ˈfɪdl] (n.) 〔口〕小提琴
10 battered [ˈbætəd] (a.) 磨損的
11 pride oneself on 為……感到自豪
12 vocal powers 在此指歌唱能力
13 clatter [ˈklætə] (v.) 作僻啪聲
14 overcome with 充滿……
15 brood [brud] (v.) 沉思；懷憂

GHOST STORIES

When the dancing was over, Ichabod joined some people who were sitting with Van Tassel, gossiping about former times and telling long stories about the war. During the war the British and American lines were close to this neighborhood, so the area was the scene of fighting. Each storyteller exaggerated his story with a little fiction[1] and, in this way, made himself the hero of every adventure.

There was the story of a Dutchman called Doffue Martling. He nearly captured a British ship except that his gun broke when he fired[2] it the sixth time. Then there was an old gentleman who, in the Battle of White Plains[3], managed to stop a bullet with a small sword. He felt it whizz around the sword, and then bounce off the handle. To prove it he could show them the sword and how it was bent a little at the handle. Several more of these storytellers were equally great on the battlefield. They all thought they played an important role in bringing the war to a happy conclusion.

All these tales were nothing in comparison with the ghost stories that followed. Ghost stories and superstitions live best in sheltered[4], long-settled[5] places like Sleepy Hollow, but they are lost when people move to big villages.

Besides, there is no encouragement for ghosts in most of our villages. By the time they finish their first nap[6] and turn in their graves[7], their surviving friends have travelled away from the neighborhood.

So, when these ghosts go out for their night walks, they have no friends left to visit.

Several Sleepy Hollow people were present at Van Tassel's house and, as usual, they were busy telling everyone their wild and wonderful ghostly legends.

They told many depressing tales about funerals and about wailing[8] ghosts. They spoke about the woman in white, who haunted Raven Rock, having died there in the snow. They often heard her shrieking[9] on winter nights before a storm.

GHOST STORIES

- Why do we find more ghost stories in 'sheltered, long-settled places' than in big towns and villages?
- Do you know any ghost stories?

1 fiction [ˈfɪkʃən] (n.) 虛構
2 fire [faɪr] (v.) 開槍
3 Battle of the White Plains
  白原之役，英國和華盛頓兩軍於
  1776 年 10 月 28 日的對戰之役
4 sheltered [ˈʃɛltəd] (a.) 隱蔽的
5 long-settled [ˈlɔŋˈsɛtld] (a.) 長久居住的
6 nap [næp] (n.) 打盹兒
7 grave [grev] (n.) 墓穴
8 wailing [ˈwelɪŋ] (a.) 鬼哭神號的
9 shriek [ʃrik] (v.) 尖叫

Most of the stories, however, were about Sleepy Hollow's favorite ghost, the Headless Horseman. They heard him several times, patrolling[1] the countryside. It was said he tied his horse up every night among the graves in the churchyard.

The church stands on a hill, and this quiet location seems to have made it a favorite haunt[2] for troubled spirits. A slope descends from the church to a silver sheet of water[3], bordered[4] by high trees. In such a sunny yard, overgrown[5] with grass, the dead could certainly rest in peace. On one side of the church there was a stream and over the stream there was once a wooden bridge. The road and the bridge itself were shaded by overhanging trees, and these made it a gloomy[6] place even in the daytime. At night the darkness was terrifying. This was one of the places where people most often met the Headless Horseman.

They told the tale of old Brouwer. All his life he never believed in ghosts, but, returning one night, he met the Horseman. The ghost made him get up behind him on his horse. Together they galloped over bushes and shrubs, over hills and swamps[7], until they reached the bridge. At this point the Horseman suddenly turned into a skeleton. He threw old Brouwer into the stream, and in a clap of thunder, he disappeared over the tops of the trees.

---

1 patrol [pə'trol] (v.) 巡邏；偵察
2 haunt [hɔnt] (n.) 常去的地方
3 sheet of water 池塘；小湖
4 border ['bɔrdɚ] (v.) 鑲邊
5 overgrown ['ovɚ'gron] (a.) 長滿雜草的
6 gloomy ['glumɪ] (a.) 陰暗的
7 swamp [swɑmp] (n.) 沼澤

Brom Bones immediately told a story of his own that was three times as amazing. He described how when he returned one night from a neighboring village, this Headless Horseman overtook him. Brom offered to race with him in order to win a bowl of punch[1]. He should have won it too because his horse Daredevil easily beat the ghost horse. But just as they came to the church bridge, the Horseman galloped away, and then vanished[2] in a flash of fire.

The men told these stories to each other as they sat in the dark. From time to time the faces of the listeners were lit by the gleam[3] of light from someone's pipe. This made a deep impression on Ichabod, who told stories from the work of his favorite author, Cotton Mather. To these he added many remarkable events. Some were stories from his native state of Connecticut, and some described the fearful sights which he experienced in his nightly walks around Sleepy Hollow.

When the party ended, the farmers gathered together their families in their wagons, and were heard for some time rattling[4] along the roads, and over the distant hills. Some of the ladies sat on horseback behind their favorite young men. Their light-hearted laughter, mixed with the clatter[5] of hoofs, echoed through the silent woodlands, sounding fainter[6] and fainter, until they gradually died away.

Soon all was silent and deserted. Only Ichabod remained to have a tête-à-tête[7] with the heiress[8], fully convinced that he was now on the road to success. What happened during this meeting I really do not know. I'm afraid something must have gone wrong, because after just a few minutes Ichabod left, looking quite upset.

Oh, these women! These women! Could that girl have used Ichabod? Was her encouragement of the poor teacher all a trick to secure her conquest of[9] his rival? Heaven only knows!

It's enough
to say that
Ichabod went
straight to the stable
and, with several hearty[10]
kicks, woke up his horse from
the comfortable bed in which he
was soundly[11] sleeping, dreaming
of mountains of corn and oats, and grassy valleys.

DISAPPOINTMENT

- What do you think happened between Ichabod and Katrina?
- Why was Ichabod upset? What did Katrina say to him?
- Ichabod thought she liked him. Why did she give Ichabod this idea?
- Have you ever been disappointed? What happened?

1 punch [pʌntʃ] (n.) 潘趣酒
2 vanish [ˋvænɪʃ] (v.) 突然不見；消失
3 gleam [glim] (n.) 微光
4 rattle [ˋrætl] (v.) 發出咯咯聲
5 clatter [ˋklætɚ] (n.) 蹕躂聲
6 faint [fent] (a.) 微弱的

7 tête-à-tête [ˋtetəˋtet] (n.) 私語
8 heiress [ˋɛrɪs] (n.) 女繼承人
9 secure one's conquest of 打贏
10 hearty [ˋhɑrtɪ] (a.) 用力的
11 soundly [ˋsaundlɪ] (adv.) 深沉地

SHADOWS

It was night and Ichabod travelled home with a heavy heart[1]. Below him from the hills he saw the dark waters of the river. In the distance he heard a guard dog barking on the opposite shore. Now and then he heard the crowing of a cock from some distant farmhouse. Close by he heard nothing except the occasional sound of a cricket[2] or a bullfrog[3].

All the stories of ghosts and goblins from the afternoon now came back to him. The night grew darker and darker. The clouds hid the stars from his sight. Ichabod never felt so lonely and depressed. In addition he was approaching the very[4] spot where many of the ghost stories once took place. In the centre of the road stood an enormous tree, which towered like a giant above all the other trees. Its branches were huge and gnarled[5] and they twisted down almost to the earth, and rose again into the air. This tree was connected with the tragic story of Major André[6]. In the war they took him prisoner close by and this tree was known as Major André's tree.

As Ichabod approached this fearful tree, he began to whistle[7]. For a moment he thought his whistle was answered, but it was just the wind sweeping[8] through the dry branches. As he came a little nearer, he thought he saw something white, hanging in the middle of the tree. He paused and stopped whistling but, when he looked more carefully, he saw that it was a branch of white wood where the tree was hit by lightning.

1 with a heavy heart 心情沉重地
2 cricket [ˈkrɪkɪt] (n.) 蟋蟀
3 bullfrog [ˈbʊlˌfrɑg] (n.) 牛蛙
4 very [ˈvɛrɪ] (a.) 正是
5 gnarled [nɑrld] (a.) 多結瘤的
6 Major André 指英國軍官 John André，他於 1775 年為美軍所俘
7 whistle [ˈhwɪsl] (v.) 吹口哨
8 sweep [swip] (v.) 拂過；掃過

Suddenly he heard a groan[1]. His teeth chattered[2], and his knees knocked against the saddle. But it was only the sound of one huge branch rubbing against another, as they were blown about by the breeze. He passed the tree in safety, but new dangers awaited him.

DANGERS

- Is Ichabod in danger?
- What is the worst thing that can happen to him now?

About two hundred yards from the tree, a small stream crossed the road. A few rough logs, laid side by side, served as a bridge over this stream. To pass this bridge was the most difficult trial[3]. Major André was captured at this identical spot. The soldiers who surprised him were hidden under cover of these trees. This stream has always been thought to be haunted, and any schoolboy who has to pass it alone after dark feels very fearful.

As Ichabod approached the stream, his heart began to thump[4]. However, he summoned[5] up all his courage, gave his horse a few kicks in the ribs, and attempted to move quickly across the bridge. But, instead of moving forward, the stubborn[6] old animal moved sideways[7], and ran against the fence. Ichabod, whose fears increased with the delay, pulled at the reins and kicked.

---

1 groan [gron] (n.) 呻吟聲
2 chatter [ˈtʃætɚ] (v.) 牙齒打顫
3 trial [ˈtraɪəl] (n.) 試驗
4 thump [θʌmp] (v.) 砰砰地跳
5 summon [ˈsʌmən] (v.) 喚起
6 stubborn [ˈstʌbən] (a.) 頑固的
7 sideways [ˈsaɪdˌwez] (adv.) 向一邊地
8 thicket [ˈθɪkɪt] (n.) 叢林；灌木叢

It was all useless. His horse started to move, it is true, but he jumped to the opposite side of the road into a thicket[8] of brambles[9] and bushes. The schoolmaster now used both his whip and his heels on the ribs of old Gunpowder, who ran forward, snorting[10], but came to a halt[11] just at the bridge, with a suddenness that nearly threw his rider over his head.

Just at this moment Ichabod's sensitive ear heard a noise by the side of the bridge. In the dark shadow on the edge of the stream, he saw something huge and misshapen[12]. It did not move, and in the darkness it looked like some gigantic monster getting ready to jump on top of him.

The teacher's terrified hair stood up on his head. What was he going to do? It was too late now to turn and run. Besides, a ghost could ride on the wings of the wind. So what chance was there of escaping from it?

Summoning up his courage and stammering[13], he demanded[14], 'Who are you?'

But he received no reply. He repeated his question in an even more agitated[15] voice. Still there was no answer. Once more he kicked Gunpowder's sides to try and make him move. Then, shutting his eyes, he started to sing a hymn.

9 bramble [ˈbræmbl̩] (n.) 荊棘
10 snort [snɔrt] (v.) 噴鼻息
11 halt [hɔlt] (n.) 停止
12 misshapen [mɪsˈʃepən] (a.) 畸形的
13 stammer [ˈstæmɚ] (v.) 口吃；結巴
14 demand [dɪˈmænd] (v.) 查問
15 agitated [ˈædʒəˌtetɪd] (a.) 激動的

THE CHASE

Just then the shadowy shape started to move, and with a leap[1] it stood in the middle of the road. Though the night was dark and dismal[2], the form of the unknown figure could now be seen to some degree. He appeared to be a horseman of massive dimensions[3], who was mounted on a powerful-looking black horse. He was neither threatening nor sociable towards Ichabod, but kept to the side of the road, trotting along on the blind side of old Gunpowder, who was recovered now from his fright and misbehavior.

Ichabod did not like this strange midnight companion. He could not stop thinking about Brom's encounter with the Headless Horseman, so he moved his horse faster in the hope of leaving the other rider behind. The stranger, however, also moved his horse faster so that he went at the same speed as Ichabod.

At this point Ichabod slowed his horse down to a walk, intending to try and lag behind[4]. But, the other rider did the same. Ichabod's heart began to sink[5]. He tried to continue his hymn, but his parched[6] tongue stuck to the roof of his mouth. He could not sing a note. The silence of his obstinate companion was very mysterious. The reason for it soon became evident.

They reached higher ground and this brought the figure of his fellow traveler into relief[7] against the sky. He was gigantic, and wrapped in a cloak, and Ichabod was horrified to see that he was headless! Ichabod's horror increased when he saw that the rider's head was in his hand.

Ichabod's terror became desperation. He rained a shower[8] of kicks and blows on Gunpowder, hoping to give his companion the slip[9] by a sudden movement, but the ghost took off[10] with a jump at the same moment. Off they went, the two of them galloping away. Stones flew and sparks[11] flashed at every stride[12]. Ichabod's thin clothes fluttered in the air, as he stretched his long body across his horse's head, in his eagerness[13] to escape.

1 leap [lip] (n.) 跳躍
2 dismal [ˋdɪzml̩] (a.) 陰暗的
3 of massive dimensions 巨大的
4 lag behind 落後
5 one's heart begins to sink
　開始失去希望
6 parched [ˋpɑrtʃɪd] (a.) 乾的
7 relief [rɪˋlif] (n.) 輪廓鮮明；突出
8 rain a shower of 大量地給予……
9 give his companion the slip
　甩開對方
10 take off 突然快跑起來
11 spark [spɑrk] (n.) 火花
12 stride [straɪd] (n.) 大步
13 eagerness [ˋigɚnəs] (n.) 渴望

They reached the road which leads to Sleepy Hollow. Instead of going up the road, Gunpowder, who seemed possessed[1] by the Devil, turned in the opposite direction, and plunged[2] down the hill. This road leads through a sandy area shaded by trees for about a quarter of a mile, and then it crosses the bridge famous in the ghost story. Just beyond that is the green hill on which the church stands.

Up to now the horse's panic gave his unskillful rider an advantage in the race, but just as he got halfway through the Hollow, the saddle's girth[3] snapped[4], and Ichabod felt the saddle slipping from under him. He seized[5] the pommel[6], and tried to hold it in place, but in vain[7]. Grabbing old Gunpowder around the neck, Ichabod just had time to save himself before the saddle crashed to the ground, and he heard it trampled[8] under foot by his pursuer[9].

For a moment the terror of Hans Van Ripper's anger passed through his mind, for this was Van Ripper's best Sunday saddle. But this was no time for petty[10] fears. The ghost was right behind him. He was having trouble staying on the horse's back: sometimes slipping to one side, sometimes to the other, and sometimes bouncing up onto the top of his horse's backbone, with such violence that he thought it was going to break him in half.

He saw an opening in the trees and began to hope that the church bridge was close. He saw the walls of the church under the trees beyond. He remembered the place where Brom Bones's ghostly competitor disappeared. 'If I can only reach that bridge,' thought Ichabod, 'I will be safe.'

1 possess [pə`zɛs] (v.) 著魔
2 plung [plʌndʒ] (v.) 衝進
3 girth [gɝθ] (n.) 馬鞍的肚帶
4 snap [snæp] (v.) 斷裂
5 seize [siz] (v.) 抓住
6 pommel [`pʌml] (n.) 鞍頭
7 in vain 徒然
8 trample [`træmpl] (v.) 踐踏
9 pursuer [pɚ`suɚ] (n.) 追捕者
10 petty [`pɛtɪ] (a.) 瑣碎的；不重要的

Just then he heard the black horse panting[1] close behind him. He was sure he could even feel his hot breath. He gave Gunpowder another kick in the ribs and the old horse jumped up onto the bridge. He thundered[2] over the wooden planks[3] and reached the opposite side.

And now Ichabod looked behind him to see if his pursuer was going to vanish, as the legends said, in a flash of fire and thunder. At that moment he saw the specter[4] standing up in his stirrups, in the act of throwing his head at him. Ichabod tried to avoid that horrible missile[5], but it was too late. It encountered his cranium[6] with a tremendous crash. He fell headfirst into the dust, and Gunpowder, the black horse, and the ghost rider, passed by like a whirlwind[7].

1 pant [pænt] (v.) 呼吸急促	5 missile [ˋmɪsl̩] (n.) 投射物
2 thunder [ˋθʌndɚ] (v.) 轟隆隆地 移動	6 cranium [ˋkrenɪəm] (n.) 頭顱
	7 whirlwind [ˋhwɝl͵wɪnd] (n.) 旋風
3 plank [plæŋk] (n.) 厚木板	8 munch [mʌntʃ] (v.) 喀喀地大聲咀嚼
4 specter [ˋspɛktɚ] (n.) 鬼；幽靈	9 uneasy [ʌnˋizɪ] (a.) 不安的；擔心的

DISAPPEARED!

The next morning the old horse was found without his saddle, and with the bridle under his feet. He was quietly munching[8] the grass outside his master's gate. Ichabod did not make his appearance at breakfast. The boys gathered at the schoolhouse, and strolled idly along the banks of the stream, but no schoolmaster appeared. Hans Van Ripper now began to feel uneasy[9] about the fate of poor Ichabod, and his saddle.

An inquiry was set in motion[10], and after careful investigation they found his trail. On the road leading to the church they found the saddle trampled into the dirt. The tracks of horses' hoofs were found in the road. Evidently the animals were racing at a furious speed. These tracks were traced to the bridge, beyond which, on the bank of the stream, they found the hat of the unfortunate Ichabod. Close beside it there was a shattered[11] pumpkin.

The stream was searched, but the body of the schoolmaster was never found. Hans Van Ripper, as executor[12] of Ichabod's estate[13], examined the bundle containing all his worldly effects[14]. They consisted of two and a half shirts, two scarves, two pairs of socks, an old pair of underpants, a rusty razor[15], a book of psalms, and a broken pitch-pipe[16]. The books in the schoolhouse belonged to the community, except for Cotton Mather's 'History of Witchcraft,' a 'New England Almanac,' and a book of dreams and fortune telling.

---

10 set in motion 開始
11 shattered [ˈʃætəd] (a.) 粉碎的
12 executor [ɪgˈzɛkjutə] (n.) 遺囑執行人
13 estate [ɪsˈtet] (n.) 財產

14 effects [ɪˈfɛkts] (n.) 財產；動產
15 razor [ˈrezə] (n.) 剃刀
16 pitch-pipe [ˈpɪtʃˈpaɪ] (n.) 定調管

Inside this last book there was a sheet of paper. On the paper, in honor of Van Tassel's daughter, were Ichabod's scribbled[1] verses. The books and the poetic scrawl[2] were immediately burned by Hans Van Ripper.

From that moment, Van Ripper decided not to send his children to school any more, observing that he never knew any good to come of this reading and writing nonsense. The schoolmaster received his pay just a day or two before. He must have been carrying all his money at the time of his disappearance.

The mysterious event caused much speculation at the church the following Sunday. Gossips collected in the churchyard, at the bridge, and at the spot[3] where the hat and the pumpkin were found. The stories of Brouwer, Bones, and many others were remembered. People shook their heads, and came to the conclusion that Ichabod was carried off by the Headless Horseman. As he was a bachelor[4], and owed no money, nobody worried any more about him. The school was transferred to a different area of the town, and another teacher took over[5].

ICHABOD'S FATE

- Do you think that Ichabod was carried off by the Headless Horseman?
- If Ichabod is alive, why doesn't he return to Tarry Town?
- What will happen to Katrina? And to Brom Bones?

1 scribbled [ˈskrɪbl̩d] (a.) 潦草書寫的
2 scrawl [skrɔl] (n.) 潦草書寫
3 spot [spɑt] (n.) 地點
4 bachelor [ˈbætʃələ] (n.) 單身漢
5 take over 接任
6 be admitted to the bar 成為合格律師
7 electioneered [ɪ,lɛkʃənˈɪrd] (a.) 參選的

A LONG TIME AFTER

It is true that an old farmer who went to New York on a visit several years after, and who provided this account of the ghostly adventure, brought home the information that Ichabod Crane was still alive.

Apparently he left the neighborhood partly through fear of the ghost and Hans Van Ripper, and partly because he was so upset by Katrina's rejection. It seems that he moved to a distant part of the country, that he taught at a school and studied law at the same time, that he was admitted to the bar[6], became a politician, electioneered[7], wrote for the newspapers and, finally, became a judge.

Brom Bones, who shortly after his rival's disappearance led Katrina in triumph to the altar[1], looked very knowing[2] whenever the story of Ichabod was told. He always burst into a hearty laugh when the pumpkin was mentioned. Some people suspected that he knew more about the matter than he chose to tell.

The old women, however, maintain to this day that Ichabod was spirited away[3] by supernatural means[4], and it is a favorite story often told around the fire on winter evenings. The bridge became more than ever an object of superstitious awe.

The schoolhouse soon fell into decay[5], and was reported to be haunted by the ghost of the unfortunate teacher. Young farmhands, traveling home on still[6] summer evenings, have often thought they heard his voice in the distance, singing a sad psalm in some secluded[7] corner of Sleepy Hollow.

1 lead sb in triumph to the altar 迎娶某人
2 knowing [ˈnoɪŋ] (a.) 知悉的
3 spirit away 消失
4 means [minz] (n.) 方法
5 decay [dɪˈke] (n.) 腐朽
6 still [stɪl] (a.) 平靜的
7 secluded [sɪˈklud] (a.) 與世隔絕的

AFTER READING

❹ Personal Response

1 Before you finished reading, did you guess how the story would end? Tell the class.

2 Did you like the ending of the story? Would you prefer the story to end in a different way? Work with a partner and together think of an alternative ending.

3 Now that you have read the story, do you think Sleepy Hollow is a good name for the place where the events take place?

4 In your opinion who or what did Ichabod love most? What did he want most of all from life? Did he achieve his ambition?

5 What did you learn about the legend of the Headless Horseman? Can you write his story?

6 At the end of Van Tassel's party Ichabod goes to talk to Katrina. Why is this meeting so important? Why doesn't the author show us this scene? How do we know that Ichabod left 'looking quite upset'? Did anybody see him?

7 If you could be a character in the story, who would you like to be?

❸ Comprehension

❽ Work with a partner. One of you reads the **A Questions**
and the other the **B Questions**. (Make sure you know
the answers to your own set of questions.)

A Questions

* What is the other name given to the town of Greensburgh?
* What was the nationality of the town's original settlers?
* Where did Ichabod Crane come from?
* How did Ichabod meet Katrina Van Tassel?
* What was Ichabod's job?
* What was the title of Ichabod's favorite book?

B Questions

* Where did many husbands tarry on market days?
* What did the Horseman of Sleepy Hollow lose and did he
  ever find it again?
* What did Ichabod do on his way home at night to drive
  away evil spirits?
* Where did Ichabod Crane go after he left Sleepy Hollow?
* What was Ichabod's job at the end of the story?
* What happened to Ichabod's favorite book and his poems?

---

❾ Work with your partner. Write four more questions
about the story. Find another pair and ask them your
questions.

10 Tick (✓) true (T) or false (F).

T F (a) The narrator of the story is dead.

T F (b) The Sleepy Hollow Boys are students from a local school.

T F (c) The Headless Horseman is the ghost of a soldier killed in the war.

T F (d) The story of Ichabod Crane took place around 20 years ago.

T F (e) The parents of Ichabod's pupils gave him food and a place to stay.

T F (f) Ichabod enjoyed reading love stories.

T F (g) Katrina Van Tassel was twenty-five years old.

T F (h) Brom Bones usually visited Katrina on Sunday nights.

11 Match these sentences from the story with their meanings.

> (1) He felt lost and without hope.
> (2) He ate everything.
> (3) He tried to escape.
> (4) All the children went home early.
> (5) He thought he was a good dancer.

_____ (a) The whole school was turned loose an hour before the usual time.

_____ (b) He managed to do justice to every dainty.

_____ (c) He prided himself on his dancing.

_____ (d) His heart began to sink.

_____ (e) He hoped to give his companion the slip.

C Characters

12 Who are these people ? Work with a partner and write the missing names.

    a He had a nickname but his real name was Abraham.
    _____

    b He wrote a book called 'History of New England Witchcraft'.
    _____

    c After he died, they found an account of the events at Sleepy Hollow among his papers.
    _____

    d During the Revolutionary War a cannon ball knocked his head off.
    _____

    e He was a Dutch farmer who used to be a mad horse rider.
    _____

13 Read the sentences below. Who do they describe: Ichabod or Brom?

    a He believes he is a good dancer.   _____
    b He wears a fur cap with a fox's tail.   _____
    c The horse he rides is called Daredevil.   _____
    d He owns a black suit.   _____
    e He has broad shoulders.   _____
    f The horse he rides is called Gunpowder.   _____
    g He has three or four close companions.   _____
    h He is thin even though he eats a lot.   _____

14 Which adjectives best describe Katrina? Discuss in pairs, giving evidence for your choices.

crafty   clever   helpful   spoilt   honest   foolish

sweet   flirtatious   well-off   kind   gracious

15 Work with two other partners. Imagine that you are a police team investigating the disappearance of Ichabod Crane.

a) Write down what questions you want to ask Brom, Katrina and Baltus.

b) Now find three students to be Brom, Katrina and Baltus.

c) Ask Brom, Katrina and Baltus your questions.

d) Discuss the answers and compare the information.

e) Tell the class what you think happened to Ichabod.

16 Who in the story might say the following words? Match the sentences with the people. Explain your choices.

Katrina   Baltus Van Tassel   Ichabod   Brom

a) 'Believe me. I know. I've read many books on the subject. I'm an expert.' _____

b) 'I'm sorry if I gave you the wrong impression. You see my heart belongs to another.' _____

c) 'So, he doesn't want to fight. That's a pity, because I'm going to make him suffer for what he is doing.' _____

d) 'What a lovely time we're all having. Don't be shy. Help yourself to some more pumpkin pie.' _____

D Plot and Theme

17 Many stories are told in *The Legend of Sleepy Hollow*. Can you complete the information about some of these stories by matching the two halves of the sentences below?

1. omens and terrible sights and sounds.
2. Raven Rock, having died there in the snow.
3. a British ship during the war.
4. against the Headless Horseman in order to win a bowl of punch.
5. his powwows in Sleepy Hollow.
6. a man called Diedrich Knickerbocker.
7. a spell on Sleepy Hollow during the early days of the settlement.

_____ a) In one story a Dutchman called Doffue Martling nearly captured . . .

_____ b) The narrator of *The Legend of Sleepy Hollow* is . . .

_____ c) Ichabod Crane told the old women tales about . . .

_____ d) They say that a German doctor put . . .

_____ e) In Brom Bones's story he raced . . .

_____ f) They told a story about a woman in white who haunted . . .

_____ g) According to another story, an old Indian chief held . . .

18 Say what happened to:

a) a certain old gentleman during the Battle of White Plains.

b) the man they called old Brouwer.

c) the soldier who was killed by a cannon ball.

19 Which of the following themes do you think is present in *The Legend of Sleepy Hollow*? Tick (✓).

_____ a Man's selfishness and greed.

_____ b The role of superstition and the supernatural.

_____ c The dangers of jealousy.

_____ d The power of storytelling.

_____ e The importance of nature.

_____ f Dreams versus reality.

_____ g The power of love to overcome all difficulties.

20 Do you agree with any of the following statements?

	agree	don't agree	not sure
a The money someone has is more important than their social class.			
b We shouldn't believe everything we read.			
c People are usually motivated by greed.			
d Educated people always succeed better in life than uneducated people.			
e Having a vivid imagination can be dangerous.			

21 What ideas or messages do you think the author wants to convey to his readers? Can you find examples in the story to support the statements in Exercise **20**?

E Language

22 Read the groups of words below and circle the odd-one-out.

- a) ginger cakes   **puddings**   doughnuts   **smoked beef**
- b) stockings   **buttons**   coats   **breeches**   petticoats
- c) pies   **apples**   peaches   **plums**   pears
- d) turkeys   **ducks**   pigeons   **bullfrogs**   geese
- e) wheat   **cider**   corn   **rye**   oats

23 Using a dictionary, work with a partner to label this picture of Gunpowder. Use the words from the box.

mane   bridle   stirrups   whip   tail   girth   reins   hoof

24 The little valley near Tarry Town is one of the 'quietest' places in the whole world. Work with a partner. Take turns to ask and answer these questions.

[a] Which is the noisiest place you know?

[b] Which is the friendliest place?

[c] Which is the most beautiful place?

[d] Which is the cleanest place?

Now, make up some similar questions of your own and ask your partner to answer them.

25 Find words in the box that have a similar meaning to the underlined words in these sentences.

> horse magic jump tales gigantic apparition prank

[a] Every little sound at that <u>witching</u> hour stirred Ichabod's imagination. _____

[b] Brom had no alternative but to think up some unpleasant <u>practical joke</u> to play on his rival. _____

[c] This legend has provided material for many wild <u>stories</u>. _____

[d] It is only fair to give you a true description of my hero and his <u>steed</u>. _____

[e] He saw the <u>specter</u> standing up in his stirrups, in the act of throwing his head at him. _____

[f] The shadowy shape started to move, and with a <u>leap</u> it stood in the middle of the road. _____

[g] He appeared to be a horseman of <u>massive</u> dimensions. _____

TEST

1 Read the questions and tick (✓) the most suitable answers.

_____ ⓐ Why is Greensburgh better known as Tarry Town?
- ① It was named after a man called Mr Tarry.
- ② The wives of that area liked the name.
- ③ On market days husbands tarried in the local tavern.

_____ ⓑ Why was it difficult for Ichabod to gain Katrina's affections?
- ① Her parents did not like him.
- ② Ichabod's rivals watched him angrily and did not let him speak to Katrina.
- ③ Katrina was spoilt and had many admirers to choose from.

_____ ⓒ What did Ichabod do when he first saw the figure by the edge of the stream?
- ① He turned his horse around and ran away.
- ② He greeted the figure in a welcoming voice.
- ③ He closed his eyes and sang a hymn.

_____ ⓓ What did the village people find when they searched for Ichabod?
- ① They found a bundle containing all Ichabod's worldly effects.
- ② They found the remains of a large pumpkin on the bank of the stream.
- ③ They found Gunpowder eating grass and still wearing his bridle and saddle.

2 Answer the questions.

ⓐ In which war did the Headless Horseman lose his head?

ⓑ What did Ichabod use to punish the troublemakers in his class?

ⓒ How do we know that Katrina was 'a bit of a flirt'?

ⓓ How did people know that Brom was visiting Katrina on Sunday nights?

ⓔ Why did Brom like to ride nasty horses?

ⓕ Where did Ichabod meet the Headless Horseman?

ⓖ Why was Ichabod so worried about losing his horse's saddle?

ⓗ What happened to Ichabod?

3 Tick (✓) true (T) or false (F).

T F ⓐ Diedrich Knickerbocker is the narrator.

T F ⓑ Ichabod instructed the children to paint and draw.

T F ⓒ Brom taught a dog to dance and introduced it as a rival of Ichabod's.

T F ⓓ Ichabod borrowed a horse called Daredevil from Hans Van Ripper.

T F ⓔ Ichabod was impressed by the huge display of cakes at the Van Tassel mansion.

T F ⓕ A group of musicians played while the party guests danced.

T F ⓖ When the dancing was over, everyone went home.

T F ⓗ Brom beat the Headless Horseman in a race and won a bowl of punch.

1 Here are some headlines from the Sleepy Hollow
newspapers after Ichabod disappeared. What do you
think they refer to?

a Missing Horse Safe

b Sleepy Residents Complain to Education Authorities

c Horseman Claims Another Victim

d Pumpkin Clue to Teacher's Disappearance

e Farmer Claims Compensation for Damaged Saddle

2 Look at some newspaper headlines on the Internet.
Invent some similar headlines of your own.

3 Choose a headline of your own or from the list
above. Work with a partner and write a short
newspaper article to match the headline.

4 In groups edit and correct the story and decide on a
suitable illustration. Bring all the stories together in
a class newspaper.

作者簡介 華盛頓·歐文，1783 年誕生於紐約一個富裕的蘇格蘭家庭。他在學校學法律，但興趣是文學。他從事律師職業後，開始為報紙和雜誌寫東西。他的文章和小說擅於諷刺美國社會的風俗習慣。紐約有很多來自荷蘭的移民，他在 1809 年出版的首部作品《紐約史》中便寫過這些移民的事。書中設定了一個叫做 Diedrich Knickerbocker 的虛構人物，全書透過其幽默的口吻來敘述。這本書受到熱烈的迴響，曾被評價為「第一本出自美國人筆下的偉大幽默文學」。

1815 年，為了幫忙打理家族企業，歐文搬到英國。但企業經營不佳，歐文於是重搖筆桿。他最有名的小說，是 1819 年出版的《睡谷傳奇》和《李伯大夢》。這些作品讓歐文在歐洲和美國聲名大噪。

歐文住過倫敦、巴黎和馬德里，他寫過小說、論文和歷史書籍，其作品像是《Tales of a Traveler》、《The Life and Voyages of Christopher Columbus》、《The Conquest of Granada》、《Tales of the Alhambra》。1832 年，他回到紐約，十年後因為外交官的身分，他再度前往馬德里。他最後的餘生回到美國紐約州的柏油村（Tarrytown）度過，這個地方就是他在《睡谷傳奇》中所設定的故事背景地點。他並在這裡寫了《喬治·華盛頓的一生》。1859 年，卒於此地，享年 76 歲。

李書簡介 《睡谷傳奇》（1809 年出版）述說一位來自康乃狄克州、名叫「奕可柏·柯鶴」教師，他來到一個叫做「睡谷」的小村落所發生的故事。他在那裡遇到了一位富有農夫的美麗女兒「嘉翠娜·凡·陶蘇」，對她傾心不已。不過他有一個很臭屁的情敵，叫做「保洪·碰司」。在女孩家中所舉辦的一場宴會之後，女孩拒絕了他的追求，他只好落寞地騎著馬回家。在回家途中，他遇到了可怕的「無頭騎士」，這是一個幽靈，是革命戰爭期間敵方的一名士兵。在一場恐怖至極的追逐後，奕可柏消失了。睡谷的居民認為，奕可柏後來也成了村子裡的幽靈。

故事的情節有諸多背景，主要故事來自頗具權威的 Diedrich Knickerbocker 的文件，他是一個虛構的荷蘭歷史學家。劇情中的戰爭、鬼故事和迷信等，則透過村民陳述出來，此外還有一些故事來自奕可柏最喜歡的《新英格蘭的巫術史》一書。

《睡谷傳奇》是美國早期小說的典型範例，主要探討的是「新生國家」這種典型的主題：這種國家擁有豐富的自然資源，人們渴求金錢和財物，可以在廣闊的土地上自由來去、追尋財富；歐洲文明的移植；戰爭在人民的記憶裡猶新；還有，過去的迷信與信仰，仍盤踞在人們的心裡。

靜謐幽谷

P.13

這個故事，出自於已故的 Diedrich
Knickerbocker 的文件。

在哈德遜河東岸，有一個叫做「綠城」
的小鎮，但一般都叫這個地方為「逗留
鎮」。這個別名是由當地那些為人妻子
的所叫開的，這是因為每到了市集日，
他們的老公都會逗留在當地的酒館裡瞎
混。但這一點我無法求證，不過為了忠
於原著，我還是如實轉述出來。

在離逗留鎮兩里遠左右的地方，有一
個四面高山環抱的小山谷，那裡堪稱是
世界上最靜謐的地方了。山谷裡有一條
小溪潺潺流過，催人欲眠，只有啁啾鳥
鳴會來打破這一片寧靜。

我記得，在我年少時，我曾經信步走
進山谷的一座小林子裡。當時是中午時
分，大地顯得異常的寂靜，山谷的一邊
樹蔭濃密。這座小山谷是遠離塵囂最好
的地方，可以靜靜地讓勞碌擾攘的生活
沉澱一下。

P.14

鄉間生活和都市生活
• 你是住在鄉下還是住在城市裡？
• 你比較喜歡住在鄉下還是都市？為
  什麼？

這個山谷長久以來都被稱作「睡
谷」，這是因為那裡很恬靜，而且和當地
居民的性格特質也很相稱。這些居民是
荷蘭移民的後代，住在這裡的年輕男子
被稱為「睡谷男孩」。在這塊土地上，彌
漫著一種慵懶而朦朧的氣氛。據說，這
是因為在殖民時代的早期，有一個德國
醫生對這個地方施了咒術。

還有另外一個說法是，有一個年老
的印地安酋長在這裡施過巫術。可以確
定的是，這裡的善良人們似乎是被什麼
下過蠱。這裡的人有著各種奇奇怪怪的
信仰，他們會進入出神的狀態、看到異
象，常常會看到奇特的東西，或是聽到
空中傳來音樂和說話聲。這一帶地方到
處都有靈異傳說，也有很多鬧鬼的地方。

而在這個靈異的地方，有一個鬼在
當家。這個鬼是一個騎著馬的無頭鬼，
有人認為他生前是個軍人，在革命戰爭
時期的一場戰役中，頭顱被大砲給炸掉
了。當地的居民常常可以看到他在黑夜
之中奔馳而過。他不僅在山谷裡出沒，
也會在鄰近地區的馬路和附近的一家教
堂裡現身。

P.15

根據史學家的說法，這個軍人的身體
就安葬在那座教堂的墓園裡，而他的鬼
魂每晚都會騎著馬，要去戰場上找他的
頭顱。有時候會看到他急急穿越山谷，
這似乎是因為他要趕著在天亮之前回到
墓園。

這則傳說，給了許多怪誕小說靈感，
而且在整個地區家喻戶曉，人們都稱他
是「睡谷的無頭騎士」。

這位為人師者

P.17

　　不只是當地的居民會「看到東西」，只要是搬去那一帶居住的人，也都會被影響到。任再清醒的人，只要來到睡谷這一帶，很快就會被這種奇幻的氣氛給感染，開始「看到東西」。在這些荷蘭人聚集的小山谷裡，所有的傳統都被保留下來。我去拜訪睡谷，是好幾年前的事了，但我可以確定，所有的事物都一如以往，保持不變。

　　約莫三十年前左右，有一個從康乃狄克州來的人，他叫做奕可柏·柯鶴，為了教育這個地區的兒童，他來到此地落腳，他稱自己是「徘徊」在睡谷裡。「柯鶴」這個名字和他頗相稱。他人高高的，身材清癯，肩膀窄窄的，手長腳長的；他的手很長，伸在袖子外面晃來晃去的，一雙腳長得像鏟子一樣；他的頭很小，頭頂很平；他的耳朵很大，有一雙綠色的大眼睛，目光呆滯，還有一個長長的鼻子。在起風的日子裡，如果你看到他在山上走過，他的衣服在風中擺盪的樣子，會讓你誤以為那是一個稻草人。

　　他的教室是一間用木頭蓋成的大房子，有的窗戶有玻璃，有的窗戶則是用舊的習字帖糊起來。教室沒有人時，就用小樹枝把門把纏起來鎖住，然後用樹椿把窗戶斜斜頂住。

P.18

　　樑上君子要闖入教室是輕而易舉的事，只是要出來時會困難些。教室單獨佇立在一座多樹山丘的山腳下，那個地點景色宜人，旁邊有一條小溪流過，一邊還有一棵很大的樺樹。

　　在催人欲眠的夏日裡，教室裡會傳出學生們嗡嗡的讀書聲，就像蜂窩傳出的聲音一樣。其間偶爾會穿插著奕可柏頗具威嚴的聲音，用語帶威脅的口氣說話；有時，在他催促慢吞吞的學生，趕緊在兩旁花團錦簇的求知之路上前進時，也會聽到樺樹棍棒嚇人的鞭打聲。

　　我不是在說他是一個冷酷的人，相反地，只有在真的遇到搗蛋鬼時，他才會動用到那根樺樹棍棒。他在體罰之後，一定會補上一句來讓自己安心：「我現在打你們，你們一輩子都會記得我，而且會心懷感激！」

P.19

　　學校放學後，他通常會陪一些比較小的男孩走回家，如果那個男孩的姊姊長

得很漂亮，或是媽媽的廚藝很好的話。他會盡量和學生打好關係，他教書的收入微薄，不夠他填飽肚子。他雖然很瘦，卻很能吃，好比巨蟒那樣可以吞下很多東西。

為了糊口，他住在學生的農家裡混些飯吃。他一個星期輪流住一個家庭，他就這樣帶著那包用棉製手巾包裹起來的全部家當，在這一帶四處借宿。

學費對這些農家來說，是一筆負擔；為了不讓農家覺得他的借宿太負擔，他會幫忙幹些活。他會做一些比較輕鬆的活，像是曬乾草、修理籬笆、帶馬去喝水、驅趕草地上的牛隻，或是砍些冬天要用的木柴。

他發現，對孩子好一點，尤其是對么子，他們的母親就會對他投以和善的眼光。他會坐上幾個鐘頭，讓一個孩子坐在他的一個膝蓋上，然後用他的另一隻腳去推動搖籃。

奕可柏還是這個地方的歌唱老師。他教孩子們唱聖歌，這能讓他多賺幾個先令。在星期天，他會帶著一組選出來的人去教堂唱歌。他的聲音會響徹教堂，蓋住所有人的聲音。

知識分子

P.20

通常，老師在女孩心中具有舉足輕重的地位。男老師就像一位擁有閒情逸致的紳士，他們的品味和專業，都遠比鄉下那些粗野的男孩出色。我們這位知識分子很享受這些鄉間女孩們所投以的微笑。星期天在教堂做禮拜的中途時間，

他是女孩們注意的焦點；他會摘墓園那邊的葡萄送給女孩們，或是大聲地讀出墓碑上的碑文，逗她們開心。有時，這群女孩們還會全部跟著他在池畔散步，看得那些羞澀的鄉間男孩只敢退在一旁；他的風度和言談讓他們欣羨。

奕可柏有點像是一份「活報紙」，把寄宿家庭的八卦消息從一家帶到另一家，所以只要他一出現，大家就會開心地跟他打招呼。婦女們認為他是一個飽學之士，因為他沿路都會邊走邊看書；他特別熟柯田·麻色寫的《新英格蘭的巫術史》這本書，他很信巫術這種東西。

廣受歡迎
- 你覺得為什麼奕可柏會受歡迎？
- 對於一心想受到別人歡迎的人，你會給他什麼忠告？

P.21

奕可柏雖然狡詐，但也很容易被騙。再奇怪的事情，他都會信以為真。放學之後，他喜歡去學校旁的溪邊，做做伸展操，讀讀老麻色那些恐怖故事，一直到天色將暗、目光朦朧為止。接著，他會穿過林子走回寄宿的農家，在溟濛時分，途中的聽到的任何一點聲響，都足

以牽動他的想像，讓他心驚肉跳。

遇到這種情況時，為了讓自己冷靜下來，或是為了驅魔，他就會唱起聖歌來。睡谷的善良居民們，他們傍晚坐在門邊時，常常被他從遠山或暗路裡傳來歌聲給嚇到。

在漫長的冬夜裡，奕可柏會和老婆婆們在一起，聽她們講那些恐怖的鬼故事。她們坐在爐火旁，一邊紡紗，一邊說著那些鬧鬼的田地、流河、橋、房子，尤其是「睡谷的無頭騎士」。

之後奕可柏也會說些巫術的事，回敬老婆婆們。他會跟她們說凶兆、可怕的異象和聲音，也會提到那些彗星和流星可能會帶來的結果，讓老婆婆們覺得很恐怖。他很喜歡這樣舒舒服服地坐在爐火旁，享受著這一切，只不過，當他要自己一個人走路回家時，就難熬了。

P.22

夜裡，雪花閃著陰森森的亮光，他走到那兒都會看到嚇人的形影。每個小樹叢都覆蓋著雪，看起來就像鬼魂，站在路旁靜候著他。連他自己的腳步聲，也會嚇到他自己。他不敢回頭去看任何東西，他怕會看到有人跟在後面。只要一聽到林木間呼嘯而過的風聲，他就會以為那是夜間出馬的騎士正在疾馳而過。

等太陽一出來，這些恐怖的事情就會煙消雲散。然而，有一天，來了一個人，使得奕可柏的生活開始受到考驗。這個人為他所帶來的災難，勝過鬼魂、鬼怪或是任何的巫師道士。這個人，是一位女子。

富裕的農家女孩

P.23

來跟他學音樂的那些學生，一個星期會來一個晚上，其中有一個叫做嘉翠娜‧凡‧陶蘇。嘉翠娜是一位富有的荷蘭裔農夫的獨生女，她年方十八，雙頰像父親種的桃子那樣，圓圓紅紅的，看起來很健美。她的個性有點喜歡招蜂引蝶，這看她的穿著就知道了。她戴著金飾，穿著短短的襯裙，這樣當她步行在田野時，就可以露出她的美腿玉足。奕可柏‧柯鶴向來就對年輕的女孩就特別心軟、特別沒大腦，所以他會對眼前這個尤物露出色瞇瞇的眼神，也就不足為怪。

嘉翠娜的父親叫老巴塔司‧凡‧陶蘇，他心裡頭只掛念著他那塊悠然愜意的農場。他的生活並不鋪張，但應有盡有。

他的房子座落在哈德遜河的河畔，那是一塊肥沃的綠野。那裡有一株榆樹，樹的枝枒在一個水質清甜的清泉上方伸展著。

在農舍的附近有一座大穀倉，穀倉的每一個角落裡都堆滿了莊稼物。燕子和岩燕啁啁啾啾地在屋簷間穿梭，一排排咕咕叫的鴿子在屋頂上享受

著陽光。肥嘟嘟的豬隻在舒適的豬圈裡齁齁叫，池塘裡有鵝，農場可以看到火雞、小公雞和母雞。

P.24

這些到了冬天就會成為美味的桌上佳餚，讓奕可柏現在看得都食指大動。他想著，鴿子可以做成鴿肉派，鵝可以做成鵝醬汁，鴨可以做成洋蔥醬汁烤鴨；豬隻在他眼裡變成了一塊塊的醃燻肉和肥美的火腿肉，火雞則變成了一隻烤雞，脖子上還掛了一串美味的臘腸。

奕可柏轉著他一雙綠色的大眼睛，對著肥沃的田野望來望去。凡·陶蘇的宅院四周，有很多小麥田、黑麥田、蕎麥田、玉蜀黍田，還有果實累累的果園，他一心渴望著的那個女孩，將會繼承這些全部的田產。他想著，他要把所有的東西都賣掉，然後全部投資在房地產上；他會把嘉翠娜娶進門，生一大堆小孩，然後他們會把家當裝上馬車，全家人一齊去旅行。他想像自己騎著一匹駿馬，向著肯塔基州、田納西州或是哪裡前進，去那裡展開新生活。

當他走進屋子裡時，他整個心都被征服了。屋子裡很寬敞，屋頂是斜式的，建築風格沿襲第一批的荷蘭移民。屋簷下堆著農具和釣具，房子的門廊這邊有一台紡紗機，另一邊則是一台攪乳器，各具功能。

在大廳裡，餐具櫥的上面擺著一排閃閃發光的白鑞器皿。在屋子的一個角落裡，放著一大袋紡紗要用的羊毛；在另外一個角落的牆壁上，則掛著一袋袋的布、玉蜀黍，以及曬乾的蘋果和桃子。

從敞開的客廳大門望進去，他看到一些雕有花紋的椅子，還有一些暗色的木桌子，桌子像鏡面一樣閃閃發光。壁爐檯的上方懸吊著彩繪的鳥蛋，在屋子的中央則懸吊著一顆很大的鴕鳥蛋。樹櫃裡擺著銀器和瓷盤。

P.25

愛情
• 你覺得奕可柏愛上嘉翠娜了嗎？
• 他為什麼想把她娶進門？

P.26

奕可柏自從目睹到這個房子和裡頭的擺設之後，就失去了一顆平靜的心，他的腦海裡就只有一個想法：要如何讓凡·陶蘇的女兒愛上自己。這比童話故事中騎士過關斬將的難度還要高。

騎士只需要對付巨人、巫師和惡龍，這些都是一些很好解決的角色；騎士只需要闖進地牢，他心愛的女士就被關在那裡。這些對騎士來說都是易如反掌的事，然後女士就會順理成章地把手交給騎士。

但相反地，奕可柏要征服的是一位嬌縱的鄉村女孩的芳心，她有很多奇怪怪的想法，讓他疲於應付。他還有很多真正的情敵，他們都很愛慕女孩，卯足全力追求她。這些情敵碰頭時總是份外眼紅，而且隨時準備對新的情敵出手。

情敵

P.27

在這些情敵當中，最可畏的對手是一個強壯、精力旺盛的年輕人，他叫做亞伯拉罕，這個名字在荷蘭文裡簡稱為「保洪」。

保洪・凡・布倫，是當地的一位英雄人物，鄉里流傳著很多他力大無窮的事蹟。他有寬闊的肩膀，動作很敏捷，留著一頭捲捲的黑色短髮。他的五官長得不差，表情有點滑稽，又有點臭屁。他有大力士的骨架，四肢很強壯，所以人們就管他叫「保洪・碰司」（譯註：Bone為「骨頭」之意）。他最出名的是他的馬術很厲害，他在馬背上的騎術可以媲美韃靼人。他是賽馬和鬥雞比賽中的常勝軍。又因為他的氣力很大，所以只要有人在吵架，他就出面主持公道，而且都是他說了算。

保洪是個粗漢，但是很有幽默感。他有三、四個死黨，他是死黨眼中的楷模。他和死黨們在鄉里間遊蕩，到處找人打架，或是四處尋樂。天氣變冷時，他會戴上一頂掛著狐狸尾巴的皮草帽子，當人們遠遠地在一群騎士中看到這頂帽子時，就會知道有人要鬧事啦。他們這票人有時會在半夜騎馬經過這些農家，一邊高聲叫囂著。老婦人們會被嚇得從睡夢中醒過來，然後喊道：「保洪・碰司他們那一幫人來了！」

P.28

他的鄰居們對他又怕又愛，而且很看好他。只要這附近有鬧事或打架的事情發生，大家就會搖搖頭，認為肇事者一定就是保洪・碰司。

保洪看上了漂亮的嘉翠娜，想追求她。雖然他的追求方式和熊一樣粗野，但嘉翠娜並沒有完全將他摒在門外。一個星期天的晚上，有人看到凡・陶蘇家的房子外頭綁著保洪的馬匹，可想而知，馬的主人正在房子裡追求嘉翠娜。其他的追求者只能失望地一路走過她家，不敢停下腳步，因為他們並不想去驚動一頭害了相思病的獅子。

奕可柏・柯鶴在和他競爭，但他是個強勁的對手。勇者會避免這一類的衝突，智者會知難而退。然而，個性既靈活又執著的奕可柏，他既有柔軟的身段，也有不凡的骨氣。他能伸能屈，只要有一點點壓力，他就懂得屈身，一旦壓力排除，就又會伸直腰桿、抬頭挺胸。

瘋了不要命，才會公開和這位情敵較勁。奕可柏並不想在愛情的戰場中落敗，所以他就採取不動聲色、攻其不備的方式。因為他是嘉翠娜的歌唱老師，所以他常常在她家出沒。他不必擔心她的父母會從中作梗，這常常是情侶們在發展感情時的障礙。

巴塔司・凡・陶蘇是一個隨和的人。他跟一般明理的男人

或優秀的父親一樣，他愛女兒，勝過愛煙斗，並且事事都依著女兒。他的太太則是要忙著家務和農場裡的活，她很清楚地看出了一點：鴨鵝不懂事，需要時時看著，而女孩們可以自己照顧自己。

P.29

天下父母心

• 一位好父親和一位好母親，應擁有哪些特質？
• 巴塔司·凡·陶蘇和她的太太，是一對好父母嗎？
• 你有什麼特別的忠告要送給嘉翠娜的嗎？

當嘉翠娜的媽媽在門廊這頭紡紗時，巴塔司就坐在門廊的另一頭抽著煙斗，而這時奕可柏會和嘉翠娜坐在大榆樹下的溪水邊，或是與她在夕陽下漫步，一派浪漫。

我不懂女人會如何墜入情網，這對我來說可奧妙了。有些女人的心扉只有一個入口，有些女人卻有千萬個入口，擄獲她們芳心的方法也是千奇百怪的。之後，奕可柏·柯鶴就勝出了，保洪·碰司好像失去了份量，週日夜晚沒再看過他的馬匹綁在嘉翠娜家的外頭，而他和這位教師之間的嫌惡也愈來愈深。

P.30

保洪喜歡用決鬥的方式來解決這場情人爭奪戰，就像古時候的騎士那樣。但奕可柏很清楚，情敵的力氣比他大，所以他不會接受決鬥的方式，也不會給對方任何的機會趁機挑釁。

奕可柏的這種和平手段，讓保洪很火大。他想不出什麼其他的辦法，就只好用一些惡劣的玩笑來對付情敵。奕可柏成了保洪一幫人欺負的對象，他以前的生活很平靜，但現在他們用各種方式來擾亂他的生活。他們將他學校裡的煙囪堵住，使得教室裡滿是烏煙；儘管奕可柏已經做了很好的學校安全措施，他們還是在半夜裡潛進了教室，把所有的東西都弄得亂七八糟。這個可憐的老師，他開始懷疑全國的巫師們都來到這個教室裡舉行會議。

惡作劇

• 什麼是惡作劇？
• 保洪一行人對奕可柏做了哪些惡作劇的事？
• 你曾經對誰做過惡作劇嗎？你是怎麼做的？

保洪會盡可能在嘉翠娜的面前嘲弄奕可柏。當奕可柏在教嘉翠娜唱聖歌時，他甚至會教狗發出哀鳴聲來跟奕可柏做對。他們兩個人誰都沒有佔到上風，這種情況一直持續了一陣子。

請柬

P.31

一個秋日的午後，奕可柏坐在教室裡盯著學生作功課，這時凡·陶蘇家的一個僕人突然來到，打破了這一片寧靜。他一路騎著馬來到學校門口，帶著一張邀請函，要拿給奕可柏，請他當晚來凡·

陶蘇家參家一場宴會。

剎時教室裡開始喧嘩騷動，學生們匆促趕完功課。能夠很快把功課寫完的學生，就不用被懲罰；慢吞吞的學生，他們的屁股吃了棍子，這樣才能讓他們加快速度，或是幫助他們認出比較長的難字。

他們沒有把書放回架子上，隨手就扔著；墨水瓶架被打翻，椅子被推倒，學校也比平常提早一個小時放學。學生們衝出教室，像一支小鬼頭軍隊往草地上奔去，鬧哄哄的。

奕可柏比平常多花了半個鐘頭來打點自己。他把他最好的那套黑色西裝拿出來撢塵——這是他唯一的一件黑色西裝；接著，他對著學校那面破舊的鏡子梳理頭髮。他要以正統的騎士風格出現在嘉翠娜的面前，所以就跟寄宿農家的荷蘭老人漢斯・凡・李伯借了一匹馬，

P.32

就這樣，他像一位遊歷冒險的騎士，啟程朝著宴會前去。

我應該將這位英雄人物和他的坐騎，做一番如實的描繪才對。他所騎的這匹馬是在農田裡幹活的馬，牠身體贏弱，而且脾氣很大；牠瘦骨嶙峋，其貌不揚，馬頭的形狀很像槌子；馬鬃和馬尾巴的毛都糾纏成一團，而且還黏著什麼東西一塊一塊的；牠有一隻眼睛已經瞎掉，看起來好像在怒眼瞪人，另一隻眼睛看起來則是有點邪門；牠的名字叫

「火藥」，顧名思義，牠以前一定是一匹很火爆的馬。老實說，牠以前可是主人凡・李伯的愛馬，凡・李伯騎起馬來是很瘋的，所以也很可能是牠感染了凡・李伯的脾性。「火藥」看起來雖然又老又弱，但牠骨子裡其實是很狂野的。

奕可柏的腳踩著短馬鐙，所以他的膝蓋抬得幾乎要比馬鞍還高；他尖尖的胳膊肘外往彎曲，活像蚱蜢的腳；當馬慢跑時，他把馬鞭垂直握在手裡，手臂的動作看起來有點像是一對翅膀在拍動；一頂小羊毛帽蓋在他的鼻頭上；他黑色外套的衣擺在身後飛揚著，幾乎飄到了馬尾巴上。以上就是奕可柏和他的坐騎的怪誕模樣。

奕可柏一邊騎著馬，一邊想著這令人愉快的秋天：蘋果可以釀成蘋果西打；玉米可以做成蛋糕；南瓜可以做成美味的派；蕎麥可以做成麵包；未來，嘉翠娜將用她那雙小小的玉手，在蕎麥麵包上特地為他塗上奶油和蜂蜜。

P.34

他帶著滿腦子的這些美味想像，一路沿著俯視哈德遜河的山坡騎去。夕陽西沉，天空上只有稀疏的幾片琥珀色雲彩，萬里無風。金色的天際慢慢轉成蘋果綠，接著再變成深藍色。

天快黑的時候，奕可柏抵達了凡・陶

蘇的農莊，他發現這一帶顯要的人物早已到齊。可以看到老農夫們穿著家裡自己做的外套和褲子，還有藍色的襪子和一雙有銀扣的大鞋子；他們的夫人戴著帽子，穿著長禮服和自己做的襯裙；現場的年輕女孩，她們的打扮和媽媽輩一樣，只是會換戴成草帽、加上精緻的絲帶，或是一襲白衣，反映出城市裡的新潮流；兒子們則是穿著短外套，外套有很大的一排銅釦，並留著當時候的時髦髮型。

色彩

• 作者運用了不同的色彩和色調來描繪人物、地點和物品，下面這些顏色分別用來形容哪些東西？

蘋果綠　銀色　黑色　白色
深藍色　金色　琥珀色　藍色

而現場的英雄人物是保洪・碰司。他騎著自己的愛馬「狂魔」來到會場，那是一匹很野，可謂「馬如其主」，只有保洪能制服得了牠。事實上，大家都知道保洪就專愛那些難馴的動物。他手下的馬什麼招式都使得出來，讓馬背上的人冒著隨時可能摔斷脖子的危險。但保洪認為，一隻乖乖牌的馬根本配不上英勇男兒。

盛宴

P.36

奕可柏一踏進凡・陶蘇的公館，眼前的景像便懾住了他。他心繫的倒不是當前美女如雲，而是各式各樣的蛋糕食前方丈。

甜甜圈、甜蛋糕、水果蛋糕、薑味蛋糕、蜂蜜蛋糕，什麼樣的蛋糕都有；還有蘋果派、桃子派、南瓜派；還有火腿切片、煙燻牛肉；還有各種好吃的蜜餞，有李子、桃子、木梨等口味；當然，還有烤雞，和一碗碗的牛奶和奶油，這些食物沒有分類地擺放在一塊。桌子中央的茶壺，壺口正放出一朵朵的熱氣。這些高檔的食物，奕可柏・柯鶴一一嚐遍。

P.37

只要有美食下肚，奕可柏整個人就會亢奮起來。他口裡一邊吃著，一邊忍不住虎視眈眈地望著周圍的美食；他一邊想著，眼前這一切的富麗堂皇，終有一日會屬於他，便不禁咯咯地笑了出來。他等著揮別教職的那一天，他要跟漢斯・凡・李伯告別，跟所有的那些小人物說再見。

老巴塔司・凡・陶蘇帶著一臉的愉悅，穿梭在客人之間。他和來賓握手，友善地拍拍他們的肩膀，開懷大懷，督促客人「不要客氣，繼續享用」。響起的音樂讓每一個人都舞動了起來，一頭白髮的樂師，他的小提琴和他一樣老舊斑駁。樂師每拉兩、三下，身體和頭就會大大地搖擺一下，身體幾乎彎得要碰到了地板；只要舞池裡多走進來一對舞者，他就會跺一下腳。

奕可柏對於自己的舞技，和歌喉一樣同感自豪。他全身上下渾身是勁，在

整個房間中馳舞，舞步霹啪響。每一個人都帶著激賞的眼光望著他，站在敞開的門窗外面，開懷地欣賞著這一幕，連農場的工人也不例外。這個向來把時間花在修理頑皮男孩的男人，此刻顯得如此生氣蓬勃、春風滿面。他舞池中的女伴正是他的心上人，他每一個愛慕的表情，都能換來女孩親切的一笑。保洪・碰司這時一個人獨自坐在角落裡，他妒火中燒，心裡頭很不是滋味。

鬼故事

P.38

跳舞結束之後，奕可柏加入凡・陶蘇一群人的談話，他們坐在那裡聊著往日時光，談到漫長的戰事。戰爭期間，英國和美國對打的戰線就在附近，所以戰爭就發生在這一帶。他們講的每一件事蹟都被誇大，每個人都加油添醋，把自己講成英雄好漢。

他們講到一個叫做大福・麻林的荷蘭佬。他差一點劫持了英國佬的船隻，只可惜他的槍射到第六發時卡住了。他們又說到在白原戰役上，有一個年老的紳士用一隻小刀劍擋掉了一顆子彈，刀劍應聲從手上彈落。老紳士可以把刀劍拿給大家看，證明這件事真實不虛，他還可以指出刀柄有個地方因此有點彎掉了。除了講古的這些人，現場還有其他人也同樣是沙場上的英雄，他們都認為自己居功厥偉，讓戰爭得以圓滿落幕。

不過，比起接下來聊到的鬼故事，這些事蹟就顯得不足為奇了。在睡谷這塊人們落腳已久的隱蔽之地，鬼故事和各種迷信特別多，而當人們搬離到大村莊後，這些事情就會被遺忘。

再說，在我們大部分人的村子裡並不興鬼故事。這些鬼魂在棺木裡初寐醒來、翻身之際，他們的生前好友已經搬離村子，所以他們在深夜夜行時，無友可訪。

P.39

幾個來到凡・陶蘇家的睡谷居民，他們如往常一樣，忙著跟大家說那些嘖嘖稱奇的鬼故事。

他們跟大家說著一些和出殯有關、鬼哭神號的淒涼故事。他們說，在渡鴉岩那裡有一個穿著白色衣服的女鬼，她在一場大風雪喪生；冬天在暴風雪來臨的前一個夜晚，常常可以聽到她的尖叫聲。

> **鬼故事**
> ・為什麼在人們落腳已久的隱蔽之地，鬼故事會比大城鎮多？
> ・你聽過什麼鬼故事嗎？

P.40

不過他們講的大都還是睡谷最受歡迎的「無頭騎士鬼」。他們有好幾次聽到他在鄉村一帶巡邏的聲音。聽說，他每天晚上會把他的馬匹繫在墓園的墓碑之間。

教堂座落在一座山丘上，那裡寂靜無聲，很適合遊魂野鬼棲身。山坡從教堂往下伸向一片銀色的池子，池子四邊高樹環繞。在這個陽光照耀、草木萋萋的墓園裡，足以令死者安息。在教堂的另一邊有一道溪流，溪流上有一座木

橋，後來繁蔭的樹木把道路和橋都遮蓋住，所以即使是在大白天裡還是顯得陰陰的。到了晚上，這一片黑暗就更嚇人了，而這也是人們最常撞見無頭騎士的一個地方。

他們還講到了老勃威的事。老勃威一向不信鬼神之說，有一晚卻在回家的路上撞見了無頭騎士。無頭騎士讓他坐在後面的馬背上，他們一路穿越樹叢和林子，越過山丘和沼澤，來到那一座橋上；這時，無頭騎士突然變成一個骷髏頭，然後把老勃威扔進溪水裡，接著一聲巨響，騎士就消失在樹梢上。

P.42

保洪・碰司立刻接著說他遇到過三次的神奇事情。他說，有一個晚上，他從鄰村返回，無頭騎士突然出現在眼前，他提議要跟無頭騎士賽馬，輸的人要請喝酒。他的贏面很大，因為「狂魔」要贏那匹鬼馬是很容易的事。然而，就在他們來到教堂的這座橋時，無頭騎士卻策馬離開，消失在一陣火光之中。

人們坐在黑暗當中，跟大家講著這些鬼故事；煙斗裡不時閃出的火光，不時地在聽者的臉上閃過，奕可柏對這個畫面特別有感覺。他跟大家分享的是柯田・麻色作品中的故事，這是他最喜歡的作家。他在故事中也另外添加許多精彩片段，有些片段來自家鄉康乃狄克州的故事，有些則是他夜裡走過睡谷時的一些恐怖經驗。

宴會結束之際，來訪的農夫們各自和家人坐上貨車。他們駛在馬路上，一直到行至遠處的山丘時，都還

傳來貨車行走的嘎嘎聲。還有些女士坐在心愛的年輕男子身後的馬背上，他們忘我的笑聲伴著躂躂的馬蹄聲，迴盪在寂靜的林間，爾後逐漸消逝。

不久，一切樓去人空，只剩下奕可柏和這位女繼承人在竊竊私語。眼下看來，他勝利在望。然而，他們言談間不知道發生了什麼事，不一會兒，奕可柏一臉怒氣地離，一定是出了什麼事情了。

哦，這些娘們！她是不是在利用奕可柏罷了？她對這位窮教師示好，難道只為了氣氣他的情敵，好讓她自己佔上風？天知道啊！

P.43

只消說奕可柏的反應，就多少可以明白。他往馬廄直直走去，對著馬用力踢了好幾腳，把睡得正酣的馬從舒適的床上挖起來，牠那時正夢見堆得像山高的玉米燕麥，和菁菁茂盛的山谷。

失望

- 你想，奕可柏和嘉翠娜之間可能發生了什麼事？
- 奕可柏為什麼要生氣？嘉翠娜可能跟他說了什麼？
- 奕可柏以為嘉翠娜對他有意思，為什麼他會這樣猜想？
- 你曾經失望過嗎？是怎麼一回事？

鬼影幢幢

P.45

夜裡，奕可柏悶悶不樂地走在回家的路上。他沿著山路走，下方是黑色的河流，對岸傳來看門狗的吠聲，偶而也會傳來遠處農場上的雞啼聲。在周圍，不時會響起幾聲的蟋蟀聲和牛蛙聲。

從午後以來聊的那些鬼鬼怪怪的故事，此時彷彿在剎那間重現。夜愈來愈黑，雲遮住了星光，景物變得更矇矓，孤獨寂寞的感覺一時湧上奕可柏的心頭。甚者，他現在正走向常常鬧鬼的地點。前路的中央有一棵大樹，高高地蓋過周圍的樹。這棵樹的樹枝又大又彎曲，往下伸的樹枝都快碰到地面，往上伸的樹枝則是高高舉向天。這棵樹讓人想起安德烈少校的悲劇下場。安德烈少校在沙場上被俘，囚禁在這附近，而這棵就被叫做「安德烈少校的樹」。

奕可柏一邊緩步朝著這棵可怕的大樹前進，一邊吹起了口哨。這時，他好像聽到有人也在對他吹口哨，後來才發現那是一陣風拂過乾樹枝的聲音。他繼續前進，看到樹的中間好像掛了什麼白白的東西。他停下腳步和口哨聲，仔細一

瞧，發現是一根被雷霹過的白色樹枝。

P.46

這時，突然又傳來一個呻吟聲，嚇得他牙齒直打顫，膝蓋碰著馬鞍猛發抖。原來，那是大樹枝被風吹拂時互相摩擦的聲音。最後他安然無恙地通過大樹，然而，前方還有不同的危險在等著他。

危險

- 奕可柏身處危險之中嗎？
- 你想，他這時可能會遇到的最慘的事情是什麼？

在過了大樹約兩百碼遠的地方，橫躺著一條小溪流，溪流上面擱了幾根並排的原木，權充做橋。要過這座橋是一個考驗，安德烈少校就是在這裡被擄獲的，士兵們當時埋伏在樹林裡突襲了他。這條溪一直都鬧鬼，男學生天黑後獨自過橋時都會嚇得膽戰心驚。

奕可柏朝著溪流前進，一顆心不禁砰砰跳。他鼓起勇氣，在馬的肋骨處敲了幾下，想快跑過橋。未料，這匹頑強的老馬沒有往前跑，卻往一旁跑去，不肯走那道「籬笆」。馬的舉動讓奕可柏更加毛骨悚然，奕可柏拉住韁繩猛踢馬。

P.47

然而馬不聽使喚，馬的確是開始奔跑，但卻是朝反方向跑去，衝進了樹叢和荊棘裡。發出鼬鼬聲的老火藥往前直奔，這位老師的馬鞭和腳後跟一齊往地

82

的肋骨處落下，牠便急急在橋邊停了下來，差點沒把奕可柏往前甩在地上。

就在這時，耳根敏銳的奕可柏聽到橋邊傳來一個吵鬧聲。他看到溪邊有一個奇怪的大黑影，黑影靜靜不動，在黑暗之中看起來像是某種大怪物，正準備撲向他。

這位老師嚇得頭髮直豎，他該怎麼辦？現在要轉身跳跑是來不及了，再說鬼會騰雲駕霧，他現在是在劫難逃了！

他鼓起勇氣，結結巴巴地問道：「你是誰？」

對方沒有應聲。他用更加顫抖的聲音問道，但對方還是沒有回應。這時他又踢了踢火藥，要牠動身，然後閉上眼睛，開始唱起聖歌。

追逐

P.48

就在這時，黑影開始動了起來，黑影一躍，就來到了馬路中間。儘管夜色黯淡，眼前這個不明怪物的輪廓隱約可見。他看起來像是一個魁梧的騎士，騎著一匹矯健的黑馬。他沒有對奕可柏做出恫嚇或是友好的動作，只是沿著路邊，向「火藥」瞎眼的那一邊奔來，這時火藥已經從驚嚇和失控的行為中清醒過來。

奕可柏對這個神祕的午夜夥伴並不感興趣。他一直想到保洪撞見無頭騎士的事，所以他策馬想甩開這位騎士。然而這陌生人也加快馬鞭，用同樣的速度和他並行。

奕可柏見狀就讓馬慢下來，以擺脫騎

士，然而騎士也跟著慢下腳步。奕可柏開始覺得不妙，他想繼續想唱聖歌，無奈喉嚨太乾卡住了，一個聲音都發不出來。這個難纏的夥伴默不作聲，非常神祕；不久，他才弄明白他為什麼不出聲。

他們來到高處，在天空的襯托下，映照出騎士的形影：他體形魁梧，披著一件風衣，駭人的是，他沒有頭！更讓奕可柏驚駭的是，他看到騎士把自己的頭捧在手上！

P.49

奕可柏嚇壞了，他對著火藥猛踢猛打，想一個快跑把鬼魂甩掉，然而鬼魂和他同時一齊向前衝，同行而奔。馬蹄下沙石飛揚。奕可柏伸直長長的身子，探到馬頭前，拚命奔跑，薄薄的衣服隨之飛舞。

P.50

他們來到了通往睡谷的路。火藥像是中邪似的，沒有繼續往前跑，而是反方向朝山下奔去。這條路經過一塊沙地，沙地兩邊樹木成蔭，那一段路長約四百公尺，接著就來到那座鬼名昭彰的橋，

然後再過去就是教堂所在的綠色山丘。

受到驚嚇的馬這麼一轉，倒是讓騎技不佳的奕可柏在競逐中佔了上風；然而在跑進山谷的半途後，馬鞍的皮帶突然劈啪斷掉，奕可柏感到屁股下面的馬鞍鬆脫了。他抓著鞍頭想拉住馬鞍，但徒勞無功。在馬鞍掉到地上之前，他抓住火藥的脖子，及時保住了小命。隨後還傳來騎士踩到馬鞍的聲音。

這一刻，他心裡浮現漢斯·凡·李伯發火的恐怖樣子，這可是李伯週末專用、最好的馬鞍。但此時沒時間想這種瑣碎的恐懼，他的身後還有一隻鬼在追他。他在馬背上坐不太住，有時滑向這一旁，有時滑向那一旁，有時在馬的脊椎上重重彈落，他覺得他到最後一定會被震成兩半。

這時樹林裡露出一塊空地，他期待教堂的那座橋就在附近。他看到遠處樹木下的教堂，他想起保洪·碰司和鬼比賽時，鬼所消失的地點。他想：「只要騎到那座橋上，我就安全了！」

就在這時，他聽到後面那匹黑馬的喘息聲逼近，他甚至可以感覺得那匹馬喘出的熱氣。他再朝火藥的肋骨一踢，這匹老馬就跳上了橋。他在厚木板上急奔，來到了橋的另一頭。

此時奕可柏回過頭，想看後面的鬼會不會像傳說的那樣，在光火和雷聲中消失不見。這一刻，他看到那隻鬼站在馬鐙上，拿著自己的頭顱，對著他丟過來。奕可柏想趕緊閃過這個恐怖的武器，未料為時已晚；頭顱擊中了他的頭，發出可怕的破裂聲響。他頭先著地的栽到在地上，接著火藥、黑馬和幽靈騎士，像一陣旋風似地消失不見。

行蹤消杳

第二天早上，有人看到了那匹老馬。牠沒有配戴馬鞍，腳下掛著馬勒。牠就在主人的大門外頭，靜靜地大聲嚼著青草。早餐時刻，奕可柏沒有現身。學童都來到了學校，他們在溪邊四處閒晃，但都沒看見老師的身影。漢斯·凡·李伯開始覺得不對勁，他擔心可憐的奕可柏的命運，也擔心自己的馬鞍。

人們開始尋人，在仔細搜索之後，他們找到了奕可柏的一些足跡。他們又在往教堂的路上找到了被踐踏在地上的馬鞍，路上還有馬蹄的足跡，可以想見當時馬匹奔跑的速度是十非疾速的。這些足跡一路朝著橋延伸過去，他們最後在橋旁溪邊的後方，找到了可憐的奕可柏的帽子，帽子附近還有一顆摔得稀爛的南瓜。

他們又沿著河流四處尋找，但始終沒有找到這位教師的屍體。漢斯·凡·李伯是奕可柏的遺物受託人，他檢查了他留下的家當包袱，裡頭有兩件半的襯衫、兩條圍巾、兩雙襪子、一件舊內褲、一支生鏽的刮鬍子、一本聖詩，和一個壞掉的調音器。教室裡的書本都是當地社區所有，除了柯田·麻色寫的《新英格蘭的巫術史》，還有《新英格蘭年鑑》和一本講夢和算命的書。

P.54

在上述的最後這本書裡頭挾了一張紙，上面有奕可柏的潦草字跡，寫著詩偈，表達他對凡·陶蘇家女兒的愛慕之情。這些書和詩稿，旋即被漢斯·凡·李伯焚毀。

從此之後，凡·李伯決定再也不送小孩子上學，因為他認為會看這些書、寫這種靡靡之音並沒有什麼好處。之前，學校老師是領日薪或雙日薪，他失蹤時一定是帶上了所有的錢。

在這件神祕事件發生後的那個週日，教堂裡大家臆測紛紛。墓園、橋、發現帽子和南瓜的地方，這些地點都有人在那裡議論著。許多人都還記得勃威、碰司等人的撞鬼事件。大家搖搖頭，得出一個結論：奕可柏被無頭騎士帶走了！因為他孑然一身，也沒有負債，沒有人會為他掛心。學校後來遷到了鎮上的另一個地點，並且來了一個新老師接任。

奕可柏的命運
- 你想奕可柏是被無頭騎士帶走了嗎？
- 如果奕可柏還活著，他為什麼不回逗留鎮？
- 你想嘉翠娜後來會怎樣？保洪·碰司呢？

許久許久之後

P.55

多年之後，有一個去了紐約、說出鬧鬼事件的老農夫，帶回來了一個消息，

他說：奕可柏·柯鶴的人還活得好好的。

顯然地，奕可柏離開睡谷，有一部分是因為怕無頭騎士和漢斯·凡·李伯，有一部分也是因為嘉翠娜拒絕了他，他惱羞成怒。他後來好像是搬到另一個遙遠的地方，在一個學校從事教職，並且另外進修法律。他後來成了一位律師，還積極參選、進了政壇，並且為報社寫文章，最後還當上了法官。

P.56

在情敵失蹤不久後，保洪·碰司終於把嘉翠娜娶進門。只要一講到奕可柏的事，他就會表現得他熟知詳情的樣子；而且只要一講到那顆南瓜，他就會哈哈大笑。有人認為，保洪知道一些內幕，只是不肯多說。

時至今日，那些老婦人仍認為奕可柏的消失是靈異事件，這是人們在冬夜爐火邊時最愛提起的話題，那座橋所代表的，也不再單純是一種迷信的恐懼。

學校不久後就荒廢了，人們說，是因為那位倒楣的老師陰魂不散。在寧靜的夏日傍晚，年輕的農場工人走路回家時，常覺得自己聽到遠方傳來奕可柏的歌聲，從睡谷的某個隱蔽角落裡傳來幽幽的哀怨詩歌。

ANSWER KEY

Before Reading

Page 8

1 a) giant b) witch c) goblin
d) ghost e) dragon
f) headless horseman

2 a) witch b) dragon c) giant
d) headless horseman e) ghost
f) goblin

Page 9

5 c, e, f

Page 10

6 a) 2 b) 3 c) 1
7 a) 4 b) 6 c) 2 d) cap, straw hat

Page 11

8 a) 3 b) 7 c) 2 d) 8
e) 4 f) 5 g) 1 h) 6
9 a) scarecrow b) fiddle c) crane
d) cradle e) pumpkins f) beehive
g) logs h) saddle

Page 15

• It was carried away by a cannon ball.
• The valley and the adjacent roads and a nearby church.
• He is searching for his missing head.
• He must return to the churchyard before daybreak.

Page 20

(possible answer) He is popular because people are impressed by the fact that he is a schoolmaster.

Page 25

(possible answer) No. He wants to marry her because she is wealthy.

Page 30

• A practical joke is a joke consisting of an action, not words.
• Brom and his friends blocked the chimney of the school, and broke into the school and turned everything topsy-turvy.

Page 34

• apple green: the horizon
• black: the suit
• golden: the horizon
• amber: clouds
• silver: sheet of water
• white: dress
• deep blue: the horizon
• blue: stockings

Page 39

Because there is no encouragement for ghosts in big towns and villages and few people have heard about the ghosts.

Page 43

(possible answer)
• Katrina refused Ichabod's offer.
• Because Katrina refused his offer.
• Katrina flirted with him and encouraged him to think that she was interested in him.

Page 46

(possible answer) Yes. He could meet the Headless Horseman.

Page 54

(possible answer)
• No.
• He is too embarrassed to return.
• They will get married.

After Reading

Page 60

8

A Questions
1. Tarry Town.
2. Dutch.
3. Connecticut.
4. He gave her music lessons.
5. He was a teacher.
6. Cotton Mather's *History of New England Witchcraft*.

B Questions
1. At the local tavern.
2. He lost his head and he didn't find it again.
3. He sang hymns.
4. New York.
5. He became a judge.
6. They were burned by Hans Van Ripper.

Page 61

10 a) T   b) F   c) T   d) F
e) F   f) F   g) F   h) T
11 a) 4   b) 2   c) 5   d) 1   e) 3

Page 62

12 a) Brom   b) Cotton Mather
c) Diedrich Knickerbocker
d) Headless Horseman
e) Hans Van Ripper
13 a) Ichabod   b) Brom   c) Brom
d) Ichabod   e) Brom   f) Ichabod
g) Brom   h) Ichabod

Page 63

14 (possible answers) crafty, spoilt, sweet, flirtatious, well-off, kind
16 a) Ichabod   b) Katrina   c) Brom
d) Baltus Van Tassel

Page 64

17 a) 3   b) 6   c) 1   d) 7   e) 4   f) 2   g) 5
18 a) He stopped a bullet with a small sword.

b) He met the ghost of the Horseman, who carried him on his horse and threw him into the stream.
c) His head was carried away.

Page 65

19 (Possible answers)
a) √   b) √   c) x   d) √   e) x   f) √   g) x

Page 66

22 a) smoked beef   b) buttons
c) pies   d) bullfrogs   e) cider
23 a) whip   b) tail   c) stirrups
d) girth   e) hoof   f) reins
g) bridle   h) mane

Page 67

25 a) magic   b) prank   c) tales   d) horse
e) apparition   f) jump   g) gigantic

TEST

Page 68

1 a) 3   b) 3   c) 3   d) 2

Page 69

2 a) The Revolutionary War.
b) He used a birch.
c) Because of the way she dressed.
d) They saw his horse tied up outside Katrina's house.
e) Because he wanted to prove he was strong and in control.
f) Near an enormous tree on the way to Sleepy Hollow.
g) Because it belonged to somebody else.
h) He disappeared. Some people say he went to New York, studied law and became a judge.
3 a) T   b) F   c) F   d) F   e) T   f) T   g) F   h) F

87

國家圖書館出版品預行編目資料

睡谷傳奇 / Washington Irving 著；安卡斯 譯.
一初版.一[臺北市]：寂天文化，2012.4
面；公分.

中英對照
ISBN 978-986-184-981-2 (25K 平裝附光碟片)
1. 英語　　2. 讀本

805.18　　　　　　　　　　101003356

■作者 _ Washington Irving　■改寫 _ Janet Olearski　■譯者 _ 安卡斯
■封面設計 _ 蔡怡柔　■主編 _ 黃鈺云　■製程管理 _ 蔡智堯　■校對 _ 陳慧莉
■出版者 _ 寂天文化事業股份有限公司　■電話 _ 02-2365-9739　■傳真 _ 02-2365-9835
■網址 _ www.icosmos.com.tw　■讀者服務 _ onlineservice@icosmos.com.tw
■出版日期 _ 2012年4月 初版一刷（250101）
■郵撥帳號 _ 1998620-0 寂天文化事業股份有限公司
■訂購金額600（含）元以上郵資免費　■訂購金額600元以下者，請外加郵資60元
■若有破損，請寄回更換　■版權所有，請勿翻印